INCRIMINATING EVIDENCE

RACHEL DYLAN

D0211760

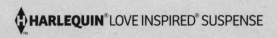
HARLEQUIN® LOVE INSPIRED® SUSPENSE

Recycling programs
for this product may
not exist in your area.

LOVE INSPIRED BOOKS

ISBN-13: 978-0-373-44756-5

Incriminating Evidence

I sought the Lord, and He heard me,
and delivered me from all my fears.
–Psalms 34:4

To my husband, Aaron.
Thank you for always believing in me. I love you.

ONE

Guilty... That's the word Jessica Hughes longed to hear after each case she argued before the jury. For now, she walked out of the Miami prosecutor's office after another long day. Although she had graduated from the University of Florida law school only nine months ago, she had a clear goal in life. Prosecute criminals and seek justice for innocent victims. And she'd known that was what she was signing up for when she had applied to work in the Florida state attorney's office. Or at least she'd thought she had a good idea of what was in store for her.

As she walked to her car in the Miami summer heat, she realized just how late it was. The sun had probably gone down an hour ago. She dug into her small pink purse, trying to locate her car keys before she got to her old black Chevy compact.

She had parked in the flat lot a few blocks away and now started walking more quickly as she was suddenly eager to get home. Even if the only things waiting for her were her orange tabby cat, Tiger, and a microwavable meal. As she approached the parking lot, she heard loud footsteps come up behind her.

Instinctively, she gripped her purse and picked up the pace. But the heavy steps hitting the pavement behind her only sped up and got closer. With each long step Jessica tried to take, the person followed her stride for stride and was gaining ground.

She was now on the edge of the parking lot, but her car was located in the middle. Fear gripped her body even as she kept moving. She'd grown up under rough circumstances. Bounced from foster home to foster home. She'd been forced to learn how to defend herself, but it wasn't something she liked doing or wanted to do right now. She wasn't a fighter—except by necessity. In fact, she'd freely give up her wallet and the five dollars she had in it.

She hadn't heard the person behind her come closer, but the next thing she knew, strong hands grabbed on to her shoulders and pushed her hard into the side of the nearest car, a large white SUV. Turning to look at her attacker, Jessica discovered he wore a dark mask.

Immediately she started to struggle against him. He was much stronger and well over six feet tall, but she refused to just sit back and let herself be accosted. Maybe if she put up enough of a fight, he would give up. *Why is he coming after me? Was this related to a case? Dear Lord, please give me strength to protect myself.* She fought off violent flashbacks from the past and tried to focus on the present.

Taking advantage of her heels, Jessica lifted up her right foot and slammed it down onto the assailant's foot as hard as she could. He howled in pain but didn't fully loosen his grip.

"Stop it!" he said, his voice deep and commanding. He reached into his side pocket.

Her breath caught. She could clearly see the knife that he'd pulled out as the parking lot lights reflected off it. He pushed the knife up toward her neck, and immediately she stilled. She could feel the pointed edge jabbing into her tender skin. The hand was poised to use the knife to slice through her throat—one sudden move and she'd be dead.

Jessica tried to slow her breathing and stay calm. She'd been through violent situations before when she was younger and untrained; now she knew better, knew more. She just had to use what she'd learned to try to stay alive.

She made direct eye contact with the man's menacing brown eyes. The only part of his face that wasn't covered by the mask. What did he want from her? Was he going to kill her right there in the parking lot?

"Please," she said. "Don't hurt me. You can take whatever you want."

He pressed the edge of the knife into her neck a little bit more, and she feared he'd soon be drawing blood. "I'm not here for your purse."

"Then what do you want?" Dread poured through her body as she tried to figure out why this man had attacked her. If he didn't want her cash, credit cards and phone, did that mean he was after her? And what was he going to do?

"This is a warning." With his left hand he grabbed

her neck and squeezed tightly. He held the knife in his right, keeping the edge of the blade against her skin.

"For what?" she croaked, barely able to get air because of his vice grip.

"You've messed with the wrong family. We won't warn you again. We know who you are. We know where you live. We know everything about you. If you want to live, you need to walk away. Just walk away."

Her vision started to blur from the lack of oxygen. Her mind tried to comprehend what the burly masked man was saying. This had to do with her work. The prosecution of Simon Hernandez. There was no other explanation. As his grip tightened, her world started to fade.

Just as she thought she was about to pass out, he loosened his grip, took a few steps away from her and then ran off into the dark of the night. Jessica stood there, stunned. Touching her neck and trying to figure out if she was actually breathing in and out. After a moment, she knew she had to do something more. But what?

One side of her knew she should call the police, but the last thing she wanted was to get taken off this case. She'd worked too hard on Simon's prosecution and wanted to see it through.

After taking a few deep breaths and walking the rest of the way to her car, she realized she had no choice. She pulled out her phone and called the police. Because if it came out that she hadn't followed protocol, that would be a ding on her record she couldn't afford as a new prosecutor. She'd just have to deal with the consequences.

* * *

FBI Special Agent Zach Taylor walked into the Miami police department at around midnight. He'd gotten called in because a prosecutor believed she'd been attacked by a member of the Hernandez organized crime syndicate. The Miami police must have thought her story credible enough to pick up the phone and call in the FBI.

Fresh out of Quantico, he'd been at the FBI field office in Miami for a month. And he'd been assigned to work the ongoing investigations of the Hernandez family. A family that was involved in more illegal businesses than he could fathom.

Of course he was working under a more seasoned agent, but the grunt work and the day to day was all given to him. It was every rookie's dream to be a part of a case like this, and he wasn't the kind of guy to back down from a challenge.

Zach was ushered back and stood outside one of the conference rooms where he would meet the victim. All he knew about her was her name—Jessica Hughes.

Miami PD detective Will Lang walked out of the room and greeted Zach.

"Nice to see you again," Zach said. He'd met Will once before, right when he'd moved down to Miami.

"If it involves anything related to Hernandez, we always call in the feds right away."

"Thank you, we appreciate that," Zach told him.

"I'm sure we'll be seeing more of each other," Will said. "There's always something going on with these guys. They have their hands in every criminal enterprise known to man, including money laundering and drugs. There's no part of Miami untouched."

"Yeah, I'm learning that quickly."

"She's all yours." Will opened another door, and Zach walked into the conference room. Seated on the other side of the table was an attractive young woman dressed in a black suit. She had long wavy blond hair and bright green eyes that focused on him like laser beams.

"Ms. Hughes, I'm Special Agent Zach Taylor with the FBI." He stretched out his hand and greeted her. She gave him a solid handshake. He examined her demeanor as he'd been taught to do at Quantico. She didn't appear to be under any duress. The only thing he noticed were the slight dark circles under her eyes.

"Agent Taylor, I don't know what all you've been told, but the FBI might be a bit of overkill."

"Don't worry about that," he said. "Are you sure you're all right? Did you receive medical attention?"

"I'm fine. I don't need to see a doctor."

Her toughness impressed him. Most people wouldn't be so calm under the circumstances. "I want to hear directly from you what happened."

She explained her attack in detail, but he had more questions than answers when she was done. This wasn't just a random woman who'd gotten on the wrong side of the Hernandez family. The fact that she worked at the DA's office added another complex dimension that he had to investigate.

"Ms. Hughes, you're working on the Simon Hernandez prosecution, correct?" She looked a little young to be an attorney—especially one working on such a high-profile case.

A deep frown pulled down her lips. "Yes. It's my primary case right now. Even though I'm a junior attorney, I've been tasked with the lead role because of some extenuating circumstances."

"I'm not making any judgments, Ms. Hughes. I'm not exactly a veteran FBI agent myself. And I can tell you that I'm here speaking with you about what happened because I'm working several investigations into the Hernandez family."

She let out a breath and adjusted her suit jacket. "Actually, it's pretty rare that a young prosecutor has this type of opportunity. We generally do a training stint when we first start at the office and then move onto two rotations in misdemeanor and juvenile court before moving onto felony prosecution. But after my training, I got enlisted to help a senior attorney on the Simon Hernandez case. I'm sure you're familiar with it?"

"Yes, I'm very familiar with it. Multiple charges of money laundering that encompass things like tax evasion and other financial crimes. Am I missing something?"

"Those are the current charges we have. At least with regard to Simon. We didn't have enough on the drug trafficking to prosecute him specifically for that, but we're using that as part of the money laundering case."

He noticed that she'd used the word *current*, and that made him think she could have something else coming down the pike. He would need to get looped in eventually because he had his own investigatory work. "So you're saying that you got brought in to help with the prosecution?"

"Yes. But unfortunately the senior attorney I was working for became seriously ill. He was diagnosed with cancer. So instead of taking the case away from me and reassigning it to another senior attorney, it was decided to let me stay on. I know the file inside and out because I've been working the case for the past six months, and fortunately the powers that be are letting me run with it. It's an opportunity of a lifetime."

This was critical information. This young lawyer sitting in front of him was the lead prosecutor in a very important case against Simon Hernandez—the son of Mick Hernandez, the leader of the powerful family. "And now the Hernandez family has found out who you are and what you're doing and they are trying to scare you off."

"Exactly. But I should tell you, Agent Taylor. It's going to take a lot more than hiring a muscle-bound thug to get me to back off. They are not going to scare me that easily. There is no chance I'm just going to walk away from this case. The Hernandez family threatens the entire city as they spread their network of crime and violence on our streets. The first step to taking them down is to get to Simon. And besides that, I've had to fight my entire life for opportunities, and something like this doesn't come along every day—especially for a new prosecutor."

He felt exactly the same about his work at the FBI. This was a time for both of them to prove themselves. But as much as he empathized with her, it was his job to make sure that she was safe and was not going to be a continued target of the Hernandez family.

"I totally understand your desire to stay on this case, but the FBI will want to conduct a threat assessment." That wasn't all the FBI would want to do, but he didn't want to scare her off right now. She already had that look in her eyes that said she was more than willing to face this threat alone, and he couldn't have that.

She threw her hands up in the air, becoming much more animated by the minute. "Agent Taylor, we can't give in to these criminals. If it's not me prosecuting the case, another prosecutor could step in. There's no way I'm dismissing the charges. This will move forward one way or another."

"But they could make it very difficult on you. I'm afraid this is probably just the beginning. Do you live alone?"

She nodded. "Yes. Well, me and my cat."

He thought about her current situation. "You're probably not in any immediate danger tonight. I'm guessing the guy who came after you thinks he got his message across. Although I'll talk to the guys here and get a police officer to escort you home to be on the safe side."

"Thank you," she said coolly.

"How far away are you from the trial starting?"

"One week."

He grimaced. That was even sooner than he expected. For some reason he'd thought it was in a couple of months. Hadn't he just double-checked the date last week? Something was off. "Did you move up the trial date?"

"Yes, at the end of last week. The defense didn't have any issue with it. I think they believe he's going to get acquitted given his power and influence in the community. They are banking on the jury being in his back pocket. And on them being afraid to find someone in the Hernandez family guilty. I can't even imagine what they're going to do to try to intimidate or influence them."

"Okay. For now I'll get you the escort home. Then tomorrow we're going to need to speak again and go over how we're going to handle this. I'll need to bring in the senior agent on the file, Brodie Wilson, and get his opinion. And I assume you have to report this up the chain, as well."

"Unfortunately, I do. It's not a discussion I look forward to having. But I'm not planning on cutting and running. They'll have to remove me from this case."

He could see that this meant a lot to her and he understood that. While they were both rookies, their work was their top priority. "Who do you report to?"

"Ultimately everyone in my office reports to the Miami-Dade state attorney, but I report to one of the chief assistant state attorneys. His name is Ian Lopez. He's one of the best, and I'm hoping I can convince him to let me see this thing play out."

"You'll have to let me know how that conversation goes. I'm sure he has a vested interest in all of this."

"How long have you been at the FBI?" she asked suddenly.

He hated answering that question because he always felt there would be immediate judgment on his skill set, but he wasn't going to pretend to be something or someone he wasn't. "I'm fresh out of Quantico."

"Like how fresh? A year or two?"

He shook his head. Might as well tell the whole truth. "As in I've been here at the Miami field office a month."

She surprised him by smiling. "Then you probably understand how I feel."

"I can relate. But I also have a job to do, and my goals may not be compatible with yours."

She put her hand over her mouth, stifling a yawn. "Am I done here? It's been a long day."

He could tell by the look in her eyes that she was exhausted. "Sure. But let me get your escort set up."

She held her hand up. "I've changed my mind. That's not really necessary."

He stood up. "Actually, it is. We can't take any risks right now." This strong-willed, beautiful woman didn't seem to realize how serious the situation was. And even though they had just met, he already felt a responsibility to protect her. Maybe it was because he understood what it was like to be starting out in his career and have something to prove.

"I see that arguing with you won't make any difference." She stood up, as well, and he could now see the very high heels she'd mentioned in her story.

"You were smart to use those as a weapon."

"A girl's gotta be resourceful."

He reached out and touched her arm, and she flinched. "I'm sorry." He quickly let go and wondered if she was sore from the attack. "But I just want to make sure you really get who and what you're dealing with here. This isn't any time to be flippant about your personal security."

"I've worked on this case for months. I know about the dangers involved."

"Do you know that once Mick Hernandez wants you dead, you're dead? No questions asked?"

She cocked her head to the side. "They have a lot of illegal businesses, but it isn't like they're ordering hits to take people out every day. You're being a bit melodramatic."

"I'm not, Ms. Hughes."

"Let's cut with the formalities. You can call me Jessica."

"All right, Jessica. And you can call me Zach. But I don't want you to discount what happened to you tonight. I know you want to prove yourself and you have a job to do, but you need to be alive to do all of those things."

"I hear you."

"Let's get out of here." He ushered her out of the room, but he couldn't help but feel as if the threat against this young lawyer was far from over.

The next morning Jessica felt exhausted. The physical attack, plus a night of barely any sleep, was taking its toll. Every time she'd closed her eyes she'd had awful nightmares about the masked man. And in those horrific dreams, he'd gone further and really hurt her.

She'd been hurt before. The scars she wore now were largely more emotional than physical, but they were ever present. She couldn't deny that the pain of her childhood had driven her to a career in seeking justice. To stand up for those victims who couldn't fight for themselves. In a small way trying to do her part. But she was afraid she might not be able to do that anymore if she got removed from the Hernandez case.

As she walked toward Chief Assistant State Attorney Ian Lopez's office, she dreaded the discussion. But she had to put on a brave face, wash away her doubts and convince him that she was the woman for the job.

His door was open, and she walked right in. Ian was usually quite informal in the office. She realized she wasn't alone. She stopped short just inside the door when she saw Zach Taylor.

The handsome dark-haired FBI agent looked the same as he had last night, wearing a similar black suit and red tie. Beside Zach was a man in a navy suit with streaks of gray at his temples. She assumed he was the senior agent that Zach had mentioned.

Ian was at his desk. "Jessica, come on in." He motioned for her to step farther into the room. He was impeccably dressed as always in a navy suit and checkered tie. Ian was a tall, slim man with short black hair and dark eyes. She believed he was seriously vying to be the next state attorney. She hoped that his ambition would work to her advantage. If he took over and personally tried the case and lost, it would tarnish his record.

"Jessica, I understand that you met Agent Taylor last night. And this is Agent Brodie Wilson."

She shook hands with both men, and then they all took seats in the chairs across from Ian's desk.

"So I hear we have a situation," Ian continued. As

always he was perfectly diplomatic. She'd call it a lot more than a situation, but it was better for her to downplay everything right now.

"Yes, sir. But I really don't believe there's any cause for alarm."

Ian frowned. "Judging by the bruises on your neck, I don't think I'd say that."

Ugh. She'd tried to use as much makeup as possible to cover them up, but nothing had really worked. "I'm doing okay."

"Well, the FBI has briefed me this morning on what happened to you and the threats that were made. I want to know how you feel about continuing to push forward with this case."

She leaned toward him in her seat. "Sir, I definitely want to keep working on it. I don't want to back down because of this incident."

Ian nodded. "While I appreciate your enthusiasm, Jessica, the FBI has some strong opinions on this."

Uh-oh. Here's where they were going to drop the hammer. She literally held her breath waiting for one of them to speak.

"We don't take threats like this from the Hernandez family lightly," Agent Wilson explained.

"I can be more careful." At this point she was going to say whatever she needed to convince them.

"That's not going to be enough," Ian replied.

She didn't like where this was going. Were they going to pull her off the case? "So what do you want me to do?" She looked at the three men and waited for one to answer her.

Ian spoke up. "If you want, you are absolutely free to step away from this case. No one would judge you here in the department. You got thrown front and center of this litigation because of Michael's illness. I—"

"Sir, with all due respect," she interrupted.

He lifted up his hand. "Let me finish. I can tell that option isn't something that would interest you, so I've worked with the FBI on a compromise."

"And that is?" she asked expectantly.

"I'm willing to let you keep working the case as the lead counsel if you agree to work with the FBI and let them provide you with the necessary security."

"What exactly does that mean?" Her mind started to race with different scenarios of how that would play out.

"You'd be working directly with me," Zach said.

"Yes," Ian confirmed. "The FBI is actually working a couple of additional angles on the Hernandez family, including a special investigation into Simon's sister, Ana. We know that it's highly unlikely we'll ever get the father because he has multiple layers of protection around him and leaves zero paper trail. But the kids are a different story. Not to mention Luke, the estranged brother who actually works for Miami PD."

Yes, she did know that there was one family member who had turned out to be one of the good guys.

"So I'm saying all of this," Ian went on, "to let you know that you'll work with the FBI closely, and maybe we can get another prosecution out of this. And you'll also be protected by Agent Taylor. It's a win-win."

She didn't really like the idea of someone being her supposed protector, but her main goal was continuing with the prosecution. She'd have to deal with whatever strings they attached to that. "But I can stay on the case?"

"Yes," Ian said. "But if at any point you want out, just say the word. I can't promise you ultimate protection and neither can the FBI. This is still a dangerous assignment. When you go to law school, this isn't exactly the type of thing you sign up for."

But that's where Ian was wrong. This was exactly what she had signed up for. Taking down those criminals that preyed on innocent people. No matter how dangerous they were. "I'm in, Ian. I won't cut and run."

Her boss smiled. "If you need me, I'm here. And I'll expect regular updates, especially since we're only days away from the start of the trial."

"Of course." As distracting as working with the FBI would be, maybe she could turn this into an opportunity. How difficult could dealing with one rookie agent be?

"Great," Ian said. "I think you should take Agent Taylor to your office and debrief him on the case and see how he can help. I'm sure then he'll have some security-related things to go over with you."

"Of course. And thank you again, Ian, for having faith in my ability to handle this case and everything that goes with it."

He nodded and stood up from his chair. "You've been a superstar since you interned here during law school. I expect nothing less than the best from you, Jessica. Keep up the good work."

His words of praise warmed her heart. It was nice to have someone build her up instead of tear her down.

"It was nice to meet you, Jessica," Agent Wilson said. "If you need me at any point, just let me know. But you're in good hands with Agent Taylor."

"Thank you," she said.

"I'll walk Agent Wilson out, so you can meet with Agent Taylor," Ian said.

"This way," she said to Zach. They walked down the long hallway to her much smaller office.

She closed the door so they could speak freely and took a seat behind her desk. He sat across from her. She had one extra chair, her desk and a bookshelf. That was it. Most of the attorneys at her level had the small offices.

She took a moment and looked at Zach more closely. Yes, there was no denying that the tall agent with the big chocolate-colored eyes and sweet smile was attractive. But it would take a lot more than a handsome face to make her trust him. Would he be friend or foe? It was time to find out. "So," she said.

"Where do we begin?" he asked.

"Before we get into the details of the case and your investigation, why don't we jump right into what you have in mind for my security."

He smiled. "You're worried about that, aren't you?"

"I like having my space." That was an understatement, but she didn't want to be too difficult. They were just starting this process together.

He leaned forward in his chair. "I can appreciate that, but I can tell you right now that's just not going to be possible."

"Exactly what are you suggesting?"

"I'm going to be your shadow."

Jessica didn't like the sound of that. "You can't be with me 24/7."

"As close to it as possible. We should discuss a safe house."

"Absolutely not. I'm staying in my apartment with my cat. Just me and him. Are we clear?"

He laughed. "Do you want to stay on this case or not?"

"Of course I do." In her mind there had to be a middle ground somewhere.

"Then, I hate to tell you, but you're stuck with me. Brodie ran this all the way up the chain to the special agent in charge of our office, Ford Cox. He's the ultimate boss in Miami, and he was very clear that we had to take an aggressive approach with your personal security."

She blew out a breath. "I don't think this is going to work."

Zach's phone rang, and he looked down. "Sorry, I have to get this."

She sat patiently while he took the phone call. Judging by the frown on his face and the serious tone in his voice, it appeared to be bad news. He ended the call and looked up at her.

"We have a problem," he said.

"What?"

"Do you know a Denise Landers?"

"Yes, she's my star witness."

"Not anymore, Jessica. She's dead."

TWO

Zach glanced over at Jessica, who was standing on the sandy beach with her gray high heels in her hand. The crime scene was currently being secured, and he wanted to get a good look at things for himself.

Jessica had refused to wait in the car, and given the circumstances he felt better having her right there close to his side. After all, that was the agreement he'd made with his boss. Zach had to commit not to let the blonde powerhouse rookie prosecutor out of his sight. Most importantly to protect her from the Hernandez family, but also because Brodie wanted to make sure Zach was tuned in to any information that she had that could help the FBI investigations.

As her wavy mane blew away from her face, he took a minute to really study her. He'd have to be oblivious not to notice how pretty she was. Not to mention that she was also bright, witty, and driven. She was the kind of woman he'd be looking for—if he were looking. But he had a job to do, and romance was the last item on his list of priorities.

Just then she turned her face toward him.

"Sorry, I know you aren't exactly dressed for a walk on the beach," he said.

She wore a gray skirt suit, but, given the blistering Miami heat, she'd taken off the jacket and removed her heels to be able to navigate the sand.

"Don't you worry about me, Zach. You're going to come to find out very soon that I'm highly adaptable."

Was there a backstory that had given Jessica such a tough exterior? He could tell from his own life experience that she was probably hiding some hurt underneath. He watched as she took a few steps closer to the water.

Detective Will Lang was on the scene and headed his way.

"What do you have?" Zach asked him.

The tall blond detective frowned. "The body washed up onto the shore and was called in by someone on the beach. But it doesn't appear that it was dumped too far out."

"Which means they wanted us to find the victim's body quickly," Zach said. It helped to verbalize his thoughts as he tried to piece together this puzzle.

"Exactly, and I don't like it one bit," Will said. "FBI is taking lead, but we're providing support in any way we can." Will's eyes shifted over to Jessica. "What's up with her?"

"It's a long story, but for now she's under FBI protection because of the threat against her."

Will chuckled. "Well, maybe you need to go back to Quantico to get a lesson on protective detail."

"Why do you say that?" Zach asked.

"Because your girl's on the move."

Zach turned around and saw Jessica taking long strides down to where the body was lying near the edge of the water. They'd covered it out of respect. He took off in a jog to catch up to her.

"Jessica," he yelled. "Wait up."

She turned around and looked at him and then kept walking. It only took him a moment to catch up to her. "What do you think you're doing? We agreed that you'd stay back until the team got done with their initial work."

She shifted her weight. "No, Zach. You told me that was what I was going to do. I never said that I'd just follow along with your bidding." She smiled at him and kept walking.

Seriously? She should know his directions were intended to protect her in any situation, but she wasn't going to take to his command easily. This woman was going to be a challenge. He grabbed on to her arm before she got too far and pulled her back, noticing once again that she flinched when he touched her.

"You can't go any further. We can't risk any more contamination to the crime scene."

"This is a public beach. The damage has already been done with all the hundreds of onlookers about before the police even made it to the scene."

"Regardless, what is it you hope to gain by getting closer?"

"I just want to get a better feel for what happened here."

He ushered her away from the body and back up the beach. "What happened here is that the Hernandez family killed Denise Landers and purposely put her body where they knew it would wash up onshore sooner rather than later."

"They had to know that Denise was the star witness for the prosecution. As the accountant for the family, she was a treasure trove of information. They take her out, and it's a much different case I'll be making. A much harder one." Jessica paused and looked up at him. "I think they also did this to send a message."

"You aren't really fazed by much, are you?" He appreciated her tenacity, but he thought she was still a bit too cavalier about her security and their investigation.

"I'd rather get to the bottom of this and then get back to work." She pushed a lock of hair out of her eyes. "The Hernandez family needs to answer for this senseless murder. The taking of a completely innocent life. Denise was doing the right thing, and it got her killed."

He watched Jessica bite her bottom lip. While she was trying to keep up a strong face, he could tell this murder impacted her. And he wanted to reassure her that law enforcement was on it.

"That's why the police are here now," he said. "They will help build a case."

"But nothing will bring her back. She's gone and that's a reality I know I have to deal with but I really don't want to face right now."

Later that evening in her office, Jessica took a deep breath as she looked into Zach's eyes filled with a bit of wariness. But she wanted to see things for herself and make her own assessments. That's why she'd tried to get a closer look at the crime scene. But with the body covered up, she hadn't been able to garner much information.

"I understand we both have a job to do here," she said.

"I agree, and that's why I think it's important for us to work together and not against each other. I get that you don't want me to be your shadow, but given you want to stay on this case and I have no alternative, we need to call a truce."

She couldn't help but smile. He did have a disarming quality about him. "Let's talk about what happened to Denise."

"This has the Hernandez family's mark all over it."

"I agree. Why don't we discuss the family? We haven't had a chance to really pick each other's brains yet about what we know."

"That's a great idea."

She nodded. "You start."

"All right. The head of the family is Mick Hernandez. Ultimate crime boss who calls all the shots but rarely gets his hands dirty. He's married to Fern Hernandez. She largely stays out of the spotlight, but my hunch is that she plays critical roles behind the scenes."

"Right, and then there's Simon. The son that I'm prosecuting. Although without Denise serving as my witness who can testify about the forgeries and money laundering given her role as their accountant, it's going to be super tough to present the level of proof we need for a conviction."

"I'll see if there's anything we can add that could be helpful given these latest developments."

"They're not going to stop until they squash this prosecution," she said more to herself than to him.

"We're not going to let that happen."

"And what about the other two siblings?" she asked. "I also have my eye on the sister, Ana. But I'm trying to focus on this case first before I attempt to build another one and charge a second member of the family. Depending on how this trial goes, though, Ana would definitely be next on my list."

"Funny you say that, because Ana is our prime focus right now."

"Then maybe we can help each other." This might actually work out after all. Especially if her prosecution of Simon got railroaded, then maybe with the FBI's help she'd be able to start working up evidence against Ana.

"Ana is dirty—there's no doubt about it. She's known on the streets as the most ruthless sibling, but she's working with someone in the organization to make sure she stays as clean as possible. But she can't hide forever."

Jessica's pulse quickened just thinking about constructing arguments against Ana. "She has a few businesses in town that she uses as fronts, right?"

"Yes, two actually. A dry-cleaning service and a restaurant."

"You know who we haven't talked about yet?" she asked.

"The only person in the family who supposedly isn't a criminal?" Zach raised an eyebrow.

"You're skeptical that the golden boy is really golden?"

"Luke Hernandez may be a cop, but I don't trust him."

She shook her head. "Everything I've researched has him coming up completely clean. The only member with zero ties to any family business or any crimes at all. Got out young and never looked back."

"Why would Mick Hernandez let his youngest son become a cop? I'm sorry, Jessica—I'm not buying it. There's an ulterior motive going on even if it hasn't presented itself yet. I wouldn't trust him."

"He works homicide," Jessica said. "Supposedly he's quite good and highly respected in the unit."

Zach laughed. "When you grow up in a family of criminals it would make you a good cop. You know all the ins and outs."

"Wait a minute. You can't judge Luke purely based on his upbringing." After the words were out of her mouth, she realized that she sounded a bit too defensive.

He leaned forward in his seat. She could tell that he was sizing her up.

"I'm sorry if I'm skeptical about Luke. I just find it really hard to believe that his father wouldn't have killed him by now if he was really an upstanding cop."

"Luke is still his son. And more importantly, he's Fern's baby. From everything I've researched, I think Fran has kept Luke off the table."

"You think even though he's gone over to the other

side and sold out his family, that his mother will still protect him?"

"That's where you have it wrong, Zach. What has Luke ever done to sell out his family? Nothing."

"Well, he better be walled off from working this homicide. Because the Hernandez clan is definitely behind the death of Denise Landers."

"Cut the guy a break. Shouldn't we applaud him for stepping out of the life of crime and all the comforts that come with it?"

Zach shrugged. "I guess if I truly believed he was clean, that would be one thing."

This wasn't going to get them anywhere. "It doesn't matter. I can tell you right now, I'm not going after Luke Hernandez. I think he's a solid cop trying to do the best he can. I'd rather keep our focus on the case I'm supposed to be trying against Simon."

"Agreed. What are you going to do now without Denise to ensure a conviction?"

"That's the million-dollar question. We do have a videotape of Denise's deposition testimony. But that's never as effective as a live witness. Plus the defense will try to exclude the testimony."

"On what basis?"

"That he lacked the opportunity for a proper cross-examination."

"How so?"

Jessica remembered that day well. "The defense attorney cooked up a story about a personal family emergency and had to leave before he could finish his questions. He cut the deposition short, and we never rescheduled because Denise committed to being available for trial. That was a big mistake in hindsight."

"And who is the defense attorney?"

"Mateo Tyson."

Zach groaned loudly. "That guy is the worst."

"But he's a very effective lawyer who has success-fully defended the Hernandez family and other crim-inals for years." She rubbed her eyes as exhaustion started to set in again.

"It's getting late. Why don't we get you home? Once we're there, we can talk about the threat assessment and the security part of this operation."

"I live in a one-bedroom apartment. I don't think that's exactly conducive to having a bodyguard." She didn't like the idea of someone invading her personal space, but there was a tiny part of her that was happy that she wouldn't be alone tonight. And that Zach would be the one protecting her. Seeing Denise's lifeless body on that beach today shook her up even though she was desperately trying not to show it.

"I can sleep in the living room. This isn't about me having luxury accommodations. It's about keeping you alive. When they sent someone to scare you, that was one thing. But now that they've killed a person con-nected to your case, we have to step it up. We'll stay at your place tonight and then regroup and talk to Agent Wilson about a safe house and any other security pre-cautions he wants to put into place."

"I have faith that I'll be all right." And she believed that in the deepest fiber of her being.

Zach narrowed his eyes at her. "Faith as in the general concept, or faith as in faith in God?"

"Faith in God."

He nodded. "I totally understand. My faith has gotten me through some tough times in life, too."

It was nice to hear that Zach shared the same beliefs. And she also knew he was right. Now wasn't the time be alone. Not when the threat loomed large. "Let's get out of here."

"Great. I'll drive you and have another agent take your car back to your place. From here on out, you're not going anywhere solo."

Jessica was quickly realizing that she was going to have to pick her battles with Zach. And this definitely wasn't something to argue about.

When she got into his government-issued SUV, she allowed herself to take a few deep breaths and try to decompress. The past twenty-four hours had been crazy.

"Are you from Florida?" he asked.

"Yeah, I am."

"Does your family still live here?"

The dreaded question that everyone always seemed curious about. Most people assumed it was totally innocent. But it was far from a benign question for her. Jessica figured that since they'd be working together she probably needed to be up front. "I actually don't have a family."

"What do you mean?"

"I grew up in the state of Florida foster care system. I was never adopted. So I don't have any family."

Silence filled the air for a moment. "I'm sorry—I didn't know," he said.

"No need to apologize. I've been on my own basically forever, so I'm quite used to it."

"I feel bad for asking you."

"Please don't. I'd like to hear about your family," she said.

"It's not exactly an uplifting story, either, although it seems like nothing compared to what you went through. My dad split when I was a baby. I don't even remember him. It was just me and my mom growing up. She had a tough time, and our relationship is rocky to say the least. We don't talk very much. It's a difficult situation."

"I'm sorry to hear that. I guess we all have our baggage." And hers just happened to weigh a hefty amount. She was relieved when he let them ride in silence. Thankfully, they weren't far from her apartment.

Jessica was jerked out of her thoughts as Zach floored it. "What in the world are you doing?" she asked. Was he trying to be some kind of hotshot all of a sudden? That wouldn't make any sense especially given how cautious his approach had been so far.

"I think we've got a tail." He gripped the wheel tightly.

"Are you serious?" She craned her neck and took a look out the back window. It was still light out, and she could see a dark Escalade approaching them quickly from behind. This was not good.

"Hang on tight."

"What are you going to do?"

"I'm going to try to lose them."

She grabbed the sides of her seat and said a prayer asking for protection. Zach accelerated again, and she turned to look back. The Escalade was gaining on them and getting much too close.

She watched nervously as the SUV closed the gap between the two vehicles. "Can you go any faster?" she asked.

"I'm doing the best I can." Zach jerked the wheel to one side, causing her body to slam against the door.

But his evasive maneuver only gave them a moment of respite. With the vehicle not far behind them, she knew there was no way out of this. The only thing she could do was keep praying. Because she realized that the person driving that Escalade wasn't just playing games. No, he was out for blood.

When the first impact occurred, she continued to brace herself. But the second time, the Escalade pounded into the back of the car just as a truck approaching them from the side came barreling toward them.

Jessica heard herself scream as she readied for a direct hit. Screeching tires and the sound of crashing metal filled her ears, and her body shook in pain. And then there was nothing.

THREE

Jessica woke with a major headache and slowly realized that she was not at home in her own bed but in a hospital. An IV was hooked into her left hand. It all came rushing back to her. The car accident—which was probably no accident at all, but another attempt by the Hernandez family to intimidate her. Unless…they were through with threats and the car crash had been meant to get rid of her.

She was alone in the hospital room, and her heart immediately sank as she started to worry about Zach. Was he okay? There was no one around for her to ask. Her heartbeat started to race, and with it the beeping monitor she was attached to.

A petite gray-haired nurse walked quickly into the room. By her side was a uniformed police officer. "You're awake," the nurse stated with enthusiasm.

"Yes, I just woke up. Where is Zach?" Jessica couldn't bring herself to ask the dreaded question as to whether he was alive. What if he had died trying to protect her?

"He just went down to the cafeteria to get some coffee. He'll be back any minute." The nurse motioned toward the officer. "And this is your security detail that has been assigned to you during your stay. But don't worry. You'll be very safe here."

Jessica let out a huge breath. She wasn't that worried about herself right now. She was just thankful that Zach was alive. "So Zach's fine?"

"A few bumps and bruises, but you got the worst of it. How are you feeling this morning?"

Morning. She must've been out all night. "My head hurts."

The nurse walked over to her. "I saw a picture of the SUV you were in. Honey, the fact that you weren't more seriously injured is absolutely amazing. The doctors couldn't believe it."

Jessica took a moment and closed her eyes and thanked God for watching over the both of them last night. From the nurse's words and the serious look on her face, Jessica understood that it could've been so much worse. "My head?"

"A concussion. Plus lots of bruising all over your body, and I'm sure you're sore. But CT scan and an MRI confirmed no internal bleeding and nothing is broken. We're giving you fluids to keep you hydrated and antibiotics to ward off infections from some of the cuts you suffered from the car metal."

Jessica nodded slightly, realizing it hurt to move to her head.

Zach walked into the room holding coffee, sporting a bandage over his left eyebrow. His eyes widened when he saw her. He approached the side of the hospital bed. "I am so glad you're awake."

"Me, too."

"Okay, you can talk for a few minutes, Agent Taylor," the nurse said. "Then she'll need to rest a bit." The nurse walked out of the room with the officer, leaving her and Zach alone.

He pulled the chair up right beside her and took a seat. Her breath caught and she winced slightly as he reached out and grabbed her hand. She wasn't expecting the contact.

"I'm sorry," he said as he let go.

"No, it's not you. I appreciate you being here." What was she supposed to say? That she didn't like anyone touching her because she was skittish from her violent past? Growing up in the foster care system, she'd lived through physical abuse. The foster parents that were supposed to protect her had ended up causing her the most harm—both physically and emotionally. And now she was understandably on edge.

"I thought you weren't going to make it, Jessica. I prayed that God would intervene. It was a direct one-two punch between the Escalade behind us and the other truck that slammed into your side of the car." His eyes showed his deep concern, and he leaned closer toward her. "I didn't want to fail you."

"And you didn't. You did what you could."

"The FBI is working on a safe house. It's too dangerous to stay at your place. Not after this. I was wrong, and I underestimated the threat against you. A true rookie mistake. But I won't let it happen again. I can promise you that."

"Please, don't beat yourself up over this." She took a breath. "But I do need some help. My cat, Tiger, will need to be fed. When do you think they'll let me out of here? And I want to take him with me if we go to a safe house. I don't want to leave him there alone."

Zach nodded. "We'll have to figure out those logistics. But there's actually a Miami PD officer at your apartment standing guard just in case the Hernandez family sent someone else. And as far as moving forward with the safe house, wouldn't the cat be happier in his own surroundings?"

Her head pounded, and it all became just too much. "I'll think about it later. In the meantime, can you just please have the officer feed him and put out fresh water?"

"Yes, of course."

"Thank you." She could no longer keep her eyes open and fell back asleep.

That afternoon, after being issued a brand-new vehicle, Zach drove Jessica back to her apartment. Once she'd been alert enough, they'd picked up right where their conversation had ended. She'd been insistent about getting Tiger and packing up some things before going to the safe house.

He was still in awe of the fact that Jessica walked away with only a concussion, scrapes and bruises. The Lord had really been looking out for her.

Zach's mom had never gone to church, so he hadn't,

either. It wasn't until he went away to college and had started attending the chapel on campus that he found out what faith in God really meant. It had changed his life forever—and for the better.

When Jessica had spoken about her faith, it seemed so natural to her. For Zach, it hadn't been a natural process but something he had grown into. It had taken him all four years of college to really find out what it meant to be a man of God. It was refreshing to see someone who had been through so much have such a resilient belief in God. When Zach had been young, he had always associated religion with wishful thinking. People wanting some supernatural force to solve all their problems. He now understood what it was to have the comfort of knowing that God was going to be with him no matter what. When he looked at Jessica, he saw something special and different in her. It made him want to know more about her.

"This is me," she said, interrupting his thoughts. "I'm on the second floor."

He pulled up into the parking space in front of her place. "Wait for me before you get out," he said.

She didn't argue and sat quietly as he exited the car and walked around to the passenger side. He was beginning to think that the attack last night had served as a wake-up call that she was really in danger.

He opened her car door and took her gently by the arm, guiding her out. She insisted she was fine to walk on her own, but he was going to be guarding her much more closely.

"Are you going to be okay to walk up the steps?" he asked.

"Yes, I can handle them. I promise you." She gave him a weak smile.

He'd called ahead to speak with Officer Lewis and make sure he was expecting them. Even though it was Jessica's apartment, he knocked on the door to be extra cautious.

Uniformed police officer Sampson Lewis answered the door. The short and stocky African American officer smiled. "Glad you two made it." Sampson looked at Jessica. "Nice to meet you, ma'am. I'm Officer Lewis."

"Thank you, Officer Lewis. I appreciate you keeping an eye on things here at the apartment and watching Tiger."

Officer Lewis grinned widely. "That cat was very skeptical of me at first. But once I started feeding him, I became his new best friend. Curled right up next to me on the couch." He looked at Zach. "It's all been quiet here, Agent Taylor. Not a peep of any kind."

"That's good." The last thing they needed was more action.

Jessica walked over and picked up Tiger. "I'm going to go start packing up a few things. It won't take me long."

After she walked to her bedroom, Zach looked at Officer Lewis. "Thanks for taking this on."

"No problem. She looked pretty banged up."

"Yeah, the crash was no joke. She's got cuts and bruising all on her face, neck and arms."

"You think it's tied to the Hernandez family?"

"Yes, unfortunately so."

"Just keep your eyes open, man. I've heard some scary stories about what that family is capable of. I have to ask you. Do you think Ms. Hughes even realizes what kind of target is on her back?"

"If she didn't before last night, I think she does now."

True to her word, Jessica walked back out of her room just a few minutes later.

"Ms. Hughes," Office Lewis said. "We just lost our cat of seventeen years a couple of months ago. My daughter is off at college, and my wife and I would be more than happy to pet-sit for you while you get through this ordeal. Tiger would be more than welcome at our place."

Zach watched her hesitate and protectively tighten her grip on Tiger, pulling him close to her body.

"I know you want to be with him," Zach said. "But it will actually be safer for him if he stays with Officer Lewis and his wife."

Jessica continued to hold on to Tiger. Zach was surprised when her eyes started to mist over. She'd been through a lot so far, but he hadn't seen her get emotional. It was clear that her pet was special to her.

"I can't just give him away," she said.

Officer Lewis walked closer to her. "Absolutely not. As soon as you're in the clear, Tiger will be ready for you. I wouldn't think of taking him from you. This is just temporary."

She nodded. "Thank you for being so kind. And my hesitation isn't because of you. I just don't want him to think that I'm abandoning him."

It hit Zach at that moment that Jessica probably felt such a strong connection to Tiger because he was the only family she had. Given her childhood, she probably had totally understandable issues with abandonment. "Jessica, if it'll make you feel better, we'll work something out and take him with us to the safe house."

She shook her head. "No, Officer Lewis is right. I need to think about what is best for Tiger. Not my own feelings."

"All right," Zach said. "But if you change your mind, you can just let me know."

She turned her attention back to the officer. "I need you to promise me something, though, and it's a big promise."

"Sure," he said.

"If something happens to me, you'll help find him a new home. A good home. You won't take him to the shelter."

Officer Lewis's dark eyes widened. "First off, nothing is going to happen to you. But secondly, you have my word that I'll personally take care of Tiger. Don't think another thought about it."

"Thank you." She held the cat for another minute and then looked back at Zach.

"All right," she said quietly. "I guess we should go."

"Don't you worry, Ms. Hughes. We'll take great care of Tiger. And we'll keep you updated." He looked at Zach. "Any reason for me to continue standing watch here?"

"No," Zach said. "Just wait for us to leave, give it a few and you and Tiger can get out of here."

Jessica didn't speak until they had been on the road a few minutes.

"How exactly am I supposed to work on the case? Are you expecting me to prepare for trial out of the safe house?"

"I'm afraid it's gotten a bit complicated where that is concerned."

"How so?"

"You should talk to your boss. But I think it's a possibility that there may be some sort of postponement."

"No! Absolutely not. That's exactly what they want to happen. We can't give in to them."

"The trial and all surrounding it isn't the FBI's call. It's your boss's decision."

"This was just a setback. It's not reason enough to call it quits. I can do this, Zach. I'm fully cooperating with you and whatever you want as far as security goes, but I need to try this case."

"I'll do everything I can to help you."

"Thank you."

"I'm taking a circuitous route to the safe house to ensure we aren't being followed." He paused. "And, Jessica, I'm sorry about Tiger. I didn't think the whole thing through." He'd touched a nerve and needed to smooth this over.

"Thank you, Zach. He's all I have, and I'm committed to taking care of him and giving him a great life."

"You're a good person, Jessica."

"I did what I had to do to survive. And I thank God that He's been by my side each step of the way—including last night in the crash."

"I can tell that your faith is strong."

"Honestly, Zach, it's the only thing that kept me going through some incredibly dark years. One of my middle school classmates invited me to church with her family, and it changed everything for me. None of my foster parents were believers, but most of them didn't mind if I went to church because it at least got me out of their hair for a bit. I know there are good foster families out there. But for some reason, I had a stretch of a few really bad ones."

He could tell the memories brought her a lot of pain. But he felt as if he needed to understand her better and give her a chance to talk if she wanted to. "Do you feel like sharing?"

"They're not good memories I enjoy talking about."

"You don't have to if you don't want to."

"No. You should probably hear this. It will explain why I have certain hang-ups. Why I chose the path of becoming a prosecutor." She paused for a while as if gathering the courage to continue. "There was some physical abuse that took place while I lived in the foster homes. Which is why I started taking self-defense classes in college. I no longer wanted to feel like a victim and wanted to be able to protect myself if I was attacked again."

"I can't even imagine." It sickened him to think about what Jessica had gone through as a child.

"Yeah, a couple of the foster parents had issues with drugs and alcohol. When they drank they got violent. In one house it was the man, and in another house it was the woman. I never could understand how a mother could beat a child—but there was one that hit both me and her own kids. It was a terrible situation."

"All I can do is say that I'm sorry for the awful pain that you went through. And to say that you haven't let those obstacles stand in your way. Your strength is evident, Jessica. And your faith shines brightly."

"It means a lot to hear you say that. I don't want anyone's pity or sympathy for what happened to me. But I've shared this with you so that you can understand why I care so deeply about my work as a prosecutor. Helping innocent victims means the world to me."

He admired her conviction. The more time they spent together, the more he grew to really like this woman. But it couldn't be more than that.

He looked down at his phone where the GPS was directing him. "We're almost there," he said, changing the subject.

"Good. My head is pounding."

"You need to rest. Once we're at the safe house, you can lie down. It's perfectly normal considering the concussion and other trauma your body suffered."

"You're probably right."

"Hang tight. We're less than five minutes out."

Jessica had crashed right after they'd arrived at their new location. They were in the middle of an upscale Coral Gables neighborhood about fifteen minutes from downtown Miami. The upstairs bedroom she was in was half the size of her apartment. The two-story Old Spanish–style house was nicer than any Jessica had ever been in. She'd expected something more low-key.

She looked at her watch and realized she'd slept for a few hours. It was time to venture out of her room and see what was going on with Zach.

As she walked out of the bedroom and toward the stairs, she heard male voices. It took her a second to realize that Ian Lopez was there. This couldn't be good.

She was careful to hold on to the railing as she quickly made her way down the stairs. She hated to admit it, but she was still far from 100 percent.

She followed the voices and walked into the kitchen, where Ian, Zach and Brodie were seated around a large table. Each man had a coffee mug in front of him. And by the serious tones of their voices, they weren't having a casual conversation.

"You're up," Zach said. "How're you feeling?"

"Better than I did before, but still sore." She wasn't going to let on to the group that her head still hurt pretty badly. "What's going on here?"

Ian looked at her. "Jessica, I was so worried about you when the FBI called and told me about the car accident. Which I understand now wasn't an accident in the least bit."

"I'm fine, though. I'll be okay, and I'm ready to move forward with my job."

"That's what I'm here to talk about," Ian said.

She needed to try to get out ahead of this before Ian went all the way down a path that would be difficult to walk him back from. "Before you say anything, you need to know that I'm able to try this case, Ian. I've been working around the clock the past two months to prepare."

He nodded. "Jessica, I'm not questioning your abilities, but I am worried about your safety. We can't have your body washing up on the beach."

She cringed, thinking about Denise. "I can finish preparing out of the safe house. Then we can have additional security for the trial. We can do this, Ian." She changed to the word *we* to make sure he felt invested in this, as well. If she was able to get a conviction, he'd look good. And if not, he'd just say it was her fault. It was a low-risk proposition for him.

"This is against my better judgment, Jessica," Ian said. "Let's proceed as if we are going to trial. I reserve the right to pull you if this thing gets out of control. As long as you think you can adequately prepare out of here, then I will try to give this another go. It's important that we don't let criminals think they can dictate how we prosecute people."

She nodded. "You're right, Ian. I'll just need to get access to a few paper files, and the rest I have electronically and can access from my laptop. One of the paralegals is working on the exhibit list, and that's almost complete." She looked over at Zach and Brodie, who had been incredibly quiet. "What do you guys think?"

"We're going to protect you," Zach said. "I don't like you being a direct target, but you two make a good point. We can't let a criminal organization determine who is going to be prosecuted or not. The legal system has to continue to function."

"Zach's right," Brodie said. "You have the full support of the FBI. We'll make sure security is airtight so you can push through and try this case."

"Thanks, everyone. I really appreciate it."

The doorbell rang, and the three men shot up out of their seats.

"Were you expecting someone?" Ian asked.

"No," Zach said.

"I'll go see who it is," Brodie said. "Zach, you stay here with Jessica."

Jessica could feel the tension mounting in the room. Was the person at the door there to try to finish the job? How would anyone have found her?

After a few moments she heard voices but couldn't make out exactly what they were saying. A few more minutes passed, and then Brodie returned to the kitchen with a man in a gray suit by his side.

He was tall and dark-haired—and looking directly at her. She couldn't shake the feeling that she'd seen him before, but she couldn't place him.

"Hello, Ms. Hughes. We haven't met, but I needed to come here to talk to you."

"And you are?" she asked.

"I'm Detective Luke Hernandez."

FOUR

Zach couldn't believe what he'd just heard. Why was Luke Hernandez standing in the kitchen in the middle of the safe house? And how had he found out the location? His mind immediately went to a possible security breach and the implications that would have for Jessica's safety.

Zach didn't trust Luke one bit. He protectively took a step closer to Jessica. "How did you find out about this location?"

"I talked to Will Lang," Luke responded calmly. As if it were perfectly normal for him to have received that type of sensitive information.

Zach shook his head. "What's the point of a safe house if everyone on the Miami police department knows the location?" A security breach like that was unthinkable. He supported the Miami PD, but they needed to get their act together quickly.

"This is completely unacceptable," Brodie added.

Zach was thankful that he and Brodie appeared to be on the exact same page.

Luke held up his hand. "I didn't come here to argue with any of you. And I can see that I'm not welcome. But I felt I had to speak up."

"About what?" Jessica asked.

Luke looked at Jessica, his dark eyes focused solely on her. "You obviously know that you're in danger or else you wouldn't be here."

"Right," she said.

"But I don't think you realize how intent my father is on making sure my brother's trial doesn't move forward. He's not going to stop until he brings this prosecution to a screeching halt. And his methods have no boundaries. He'll persevere until his goal is reached no matter what the cost or the collateral damage along the way."

"And you needed to come here in person to tell us something we already knew?" Zach asked. He wasn't buying any of this coming from Luke. There was something else going on here.

"No. But I did want to tell you that it's only a matter of time. I give it forty-eight hours max before the people that work for my family find this house. You're not safe here for long. You need to go off the grid."

"I'm not going to do that," Jessica said, her voice louder than normal. "I'm going to move forward with this case."

Luke nodded. "I figured you'd say that, but I thought the more information you had the better. And that maybe the FBI could be more cautious given the circumstances."

"What's your angle in all of this?" Ian spoke up.

"It's no secret that I'm the only member of my family who hasn't chosen a life of crime. And I hate to see innocent people hurt. It's one of the reasons I became a cop. If there's something I can do to help Ms. Hughes, I intend to do it." He paused and looked directly at Zach. "Even if my assistance isn't wanted."

"Thank you, Luke," Jessica said. "I think it's an admirable decision you made to go against your family and get into law enforcement. And since I'm the target here, I'm happy to have your help."

Luke nodded. "If there's anything I can do, please don't hesitate to ask."

Brodie took a step toward Luke. "I understand that you think you're helping the situation here, but from now on it would probably be better if you let the FBI handle it." Brodie handed Luke his business card. "You can call me if you have any pertinent information to relay."

Zach was relieved that Brodie had stepped up. Zach didn't like how Luke had taken a special interest in Jessica.

"I can see myself out," Luke said. It was clear he wasn't interested in engaging in any arguments.

After Luke walked out of the room, silence remained until Brodie spoke up. "Even if he *is* law enforcement, I don't like the fact that Will Lang divulged the location of the safe house to him. Unfortunately, we don't have a better alternative right now. I'm going to have extra security posted outside just in case there is any further breach of protocol. We already had an on-call team, so I'll have them come over now." Brodie pulled out his phone to text the team.

Zach nodded. "I think that's a good idea. Then we can reevaluate our options tomorrow." Zach could tell by the frown on Jessica's face that she was still bothered by the Luke situation. He turned toward her. "I'm sorry if that seemed rude with how we handled Luke, but we aren't in a position to be taking chances right now."

She looked up at him. "You have absolutely no evidence that Luke isn't one of the good guys. He took a risk just by coming here to try to help me. So I think all of you should just cut the poor guy some slack and back off. He's not the enemy we're facing. Let's not forget that."

Zach looked at his watch. "I'm sorry to have upset you, but we're trying to do the job to the best of our ability."

"I understand that," she said softly.

"I know you must be hungry." He made an effort to change the subject and defuse the tense situation. "We've got an agent bringing food in about half an hour."

"That would be great. Now that you mention it, I'm starving."

"Jessica, I think you have your marching orders," Ian chimed in. "The plan will be to start the trial on schedule. You're well on your way with all the prep work you've done. Let's push through and get this thing done."

"That won't be an issue, Ian," she said. "Thanks for bringing me a laptop to work on."

Jessica would be able to access her files and prepare her case from the remote location. Zach's main concern was what was going to happen once the trial started. He felt that he could keep her out of danger in the cocoon that was the safe house, but outside of it was another story.

"If you need anything, you know where to find me," Ian said. Then he turned and looked at Zach. "I'm entrusting her security to you."

"I understand," Zach said.

Brodie stayed with them until he got the confirmation that the protective detail had arrived. "I'll head out, too," Brodie said. "Everything should be all set here."

Between the complex high-tech security system and the extra security posted outside, Zach was confident they were well protected. Much better than he would've felt at Jessica's apartment. This was the first time he'd ever done this type of work, but he was catching on quickly and having Brodie's confidence in him helped build his own.

It wasn't long before one of the agents delivered their dinner, a combination of Thai food that he and Jessica had no trouble putting away quickly. As they sat at the kitchen table after the meal, he took a moment to assess how she was doing.

"How are you feeling?" he asked.

"Besides the headache that won't seem to go away, I'm doing all right."

It was obvious to him that she was still in pain. "Maybe a good night's rest will help."

"Tomorrow's Thursday. I need to get in a full day of work. The trial starts Monday."

"What can I do to help?"

She pushed her hair behind her ear and leaned back in the chair. "As long as you're focused on making sure no one attacks us, I can handle the legal work."

"I've got the security element covered."

"Good. Now I have to figure out how to make this case against Simon with only the limited video deposition testimony from Denise. And if the judge disallows the recorded testimony, then I'm really in a world of hurt."

"You always need a backup plan." Something they had drilled into his head from day one at Quantico.

"In an ideal world, but unfortunately my backup plan is flimsy and purely circumstantial evidence. Any defense attorney who knows what he's doing will tear that apart. And Mateo Tyson is one of the best. It's tough preparing for a battle that you feel like you don't have the ammunition to fight. And knowing that the reason for that is because the Hernandez family got rid of my main witness. It seems so wrong to me, but I can't bring up the fact at trial that my star witness was murdered. The judge won't allow that because it's too prejudicial to the defense. I won't be able to explain to the jury why the witness isn't testifying in person."

He could see that she was at a low point, and it bothered him that he couldn't just fix the situation. "You can't feel defeated before you even start. There's always a way, Jessica. You just have to find it."

"Aren't you the optimist?"

"I believe that half of our battles in life take place in the mind. If you psych yourself out, you'll set yourself up for failure. You have to believe that a jury will convict Simon. If you walk in there with your tail between your legs, the jury will sense your lack of confidence from day one. I don't want to see that happen."

She leaned back in her chair again. "I understand your point, but I think it's better to be realistic. I'm going to do my absolute best to get a conviction, but I have to go to trial with the evidence I have. I can't change it. No amount of positive thinking will bring Denise back. The type of testimony she could've provided as one of the top accountants for the Hernandez family would've been invaluable. She had access to all the financial records." She paused. "She was a nice woman. A brave woman who was taking a stand against them. She most certainly didn't deserve this. If only I could've done more to protect her."

"I'm sorry." He thought for a minute. "Why wasn't she under some sort of security detail?"

Jessica looked down and then back up at him. "I tried to talk her into it. But she refused. I don't think she thought that they'd actually hurt her. Scare her maybe, but not this. It's awful. I should've been more insistent with her. If I hadn't given up on trying to convince her to take the security detail, then she'd still be here."

"It was ultimately her choice, Jessica. You can't put that burden on yourself."

She nodded but didn't say anything.

"It's a stark reminder of the threat that you're still facing."

She rubbed her temples as she stood up from the chair. "I'm going to turn in. Tomorrow will be a busy day of trial preparation."

* * *

Loud screams woke Zach from his sleep. He'd decided to get a few minutes of shut-eye because the house was totally locked down, and he knew he needed rest to be able to function at the highest level possible. But now he was wide-awake and was rushing up the stairs. What if someone had gotten inside? And he'd been asleep, leaving Jessica defenseless? The recriminations would have to wait for later.

Adrenaline pumped through his veins as he took the steps two at a time and then launched toward the second room on the right where Jessica was staying. She was still screaming as he threw open the door and drew his gun—ready to face whatever threat was lurking.

He flipped on the light and saw that no one was there. Jessica sat up in the bed, her eyes open and staring at him wildly.

Zach lowered his gun immediately. "Jessica, are you okay?" he asked.

He saw that there was sweat around her hairline and her skin was flushed. She was taking in shallow breaths, and she didn't immediately respond to him. He became even more concerned. He took a step toward her, and she recoiled. He stopped. He could tell she was in a state of shock, but the psychological stuff wasn't his strong suit. Zach would almost rather it have been a physical threat. That he could've handled. He'd aced the physical stuff at Quantico, but not so much the behavioral psychology classes.

Still, he hated feeling helpless in the situation. He

wanted some way to be able to help this strong, independent woman he'd come to admire.

Slowly he took a step toward her. "Jessica, I think you were having a bad nightmare. But you're totally safe now. Do you understand?"

Her shoulders visibly relaxed. "A nightmare," she repeated softly.

"Yes, it was just a bad dream. There's no one here to harm you. It's just us, and I'm not going to let anything happen to you."

She ran her fingers through her tousled hair. "I'm sorry. I feel so embarrassed."

He took another step toward her and knelt down beside the bed. "You have absolutely nothing to apologize for. If you didn't have any reaction to all that has happened to you over the past couple of days, then I'd think something was wrong with you."

She smiled. "You and I both know that this is about more than just the past couple of days. I'm messed up. You understand that there's more going on with me than meets the eye."

"One second." He stood up and went to the bathroom that connected to her room and got a cool washcloth. He thought she might want a second to collect herself. For that matter, he needed a moment, too. When he walked back into the room, she no longer had a look of fear in her eyes.

"Here you go." He handed her the washcloth. He knew better than to try to touch her. Especially after the nightmare. He was beginning to understand just how deep her issues went.

"Thank you." She took the washcloth and patted it against her face. "Well, I'm making your first assignment as an FBI agent pretty interesting."

He smiled. "You're doing great. I can deal with the nightmares." He didn't want her to think that he couldn't handle the situation even if it did push him out of his comfort zone.

"How many psych classes did you take at Quantico? Because you probably need those the most when dealing with me. I'm not your normal case—that's for sure."

She was trying to make light of the situation, but he could tell how deeply this all bothered her. And he wanted to be able to help in some way. "Do you want to talk about the dream? Would that help or make it worse?"

"I have recurring nightmares. That's nothing new. But this one tonight was more sinister, and it felt so real. I couldn't see the man's face, but he cornered me in a dark alley. And he was literally squeezing the breath out of me. I could feel the life slipping out of my body. Death seemed so certain."

"Well, that sounds directly connected to the first attack against you. I don't think that's strange at all for you to be reliving that experience."

"You're right. It's probably reasonable, but the visceral reactions aren't. I can tell you're a smart guy. You've figured out that I have a problem being touched. Physical contact often bothers me. Imagine trying to go through life like that."

He had noticed and had connected the dots that it had to be related to the abuse she had faced as a child. He couldn't even fathom what she'd gone through. "Have you talked to a doctor about it?"

"You mean like a psychiatrist?"

"Or something similar."

"I did a lot of therapy through college. But I learned that the counseling, while it was necessary to help me get through those initial years after I left foster care, was repetitive after a while. I felt like I was saying the same thing over and over—reliving the trauma over and over. It was necessary to work through it, but once that had happened, it wasn't really that helpful for me. I miss having Tiger with me. He provides a lot of comfort in these situations."

"I'm sorry. If you want us to get him, we can."

"No. I don't want to put him in any danger. I'll have to tough it out."

"Let me know if you change your mind."

"My relationship with God is really what has pulled me through. It would've been easy to drop into a deep abyss of depression and never come out of it."

"I've learned that God has a way of coming through for us when we need it the most. My last year of college my mom was totally going off the deep end. I felt bad, so I went to visit her, but it was literally one of the toughest experiences of my life. She was so strung out she barely knew who I was. But the sad thing is that she didn't want any help from me. In that moment of feeling so weak and helpless, I turned to God for strength because honestly I didn't think I had enough to get me through."

"It is amazing what He is able to do. What is your relationship with your mother like now?"

"That's a difficult question to answer. To say we even have one might be a little bit of a stretch. Things are uneven—let's put it that way."

"You speak very diplomatically. Are you sure you don't have your sights set on running for office one day?"

He laughed. "I can honestly say that is not in my game plan."

"What are your career goals?"

He could tell that she wanted to talk about something unrelated to the case to distance herself from what she'd just experienced. "I think most FBI agents who have ambition would love to run their own office and be a special agent in charge. But I know I have to put in years of service before that would even be on the table. I'm excited about learning the different areas that we investigate, though."

"You definitely started with a very exciting one. If you get thrown into insurance fraud or something next, it will be a big letdown."

He grinned. "You've got that right. But I have to take the thrilling assignments with the more mundane."

"Yeah, paying dues and all of that."

"We both got thrown into cases that we normally wouldn't see for years." It was a strong common bond between them.

"I know. Which is why this is so important to me." She paused. "What time is it?"

He looked down at his watch. "It's about five a.m."

"I should get up. I don't think I'm going to be able to go back to sleep. I can start working."

"Whatever you want to do." He didn't think he was in any position to go back to sleep, either. Might as well face the day.

"First I'm going to make coffee so that my brain can start to function."

"Please make a big pot." He laughed.

"Seriously, Zach. Thanks for talking with me. I feel a lot better now."

His heart warmed as he looked into her eyes. He was drawn to her. So vulnerable and yet so strong at the same time. "Of course." He stood up. "I'll let you get ready."

He walked out of her room and closed the door. And he wondered if he was starting to care about Jessica more than he should.

Jessica had turned the large dining room table into her desk. She had her laptop, legal pads and a lot of Post-it notes. Zach had largely left her alone to do her thing. But he would check on her every couple of hours. It was now late afternoon, and she was hitting a wall.

After the restless night filled with awful dreams, she felt completely drained. She also couldn't believe that she'd shown such a raw and tender part of herself to Zach. She always tried so hard to put up a tough front—big walls to protect her from all the evils of the world—but Zach had seen firsthand how damaged she really was.

Even though she didn't want to admit it, she knew

deep down that Zach was special. He had vowed to protect her, and she actually believed him. But it was more. A strange thought crept into her mind: Was it possible that she could think of Zach as more than just her protector? The idea scared her, but it also gave her a tiny shred of hope that she might be able to break away from her fears and pain and find happiness.

But that was something to think about later. She still had a vitally important job to do. She couldn't believe that this trial was actually going to start on Monday. It seemed surreal. At this point, she was thankful she'd put in those ridiculously long hours the past two months because even though she had stuff to do to prepare, she was actually in good shape. It took some of the pressure off and allowed her to focus on the strategy adjustments now that she had to make the case without Denise.

Taking a deep breath, she tried to engage in the positive visualization trial techniques that her law school professor had taught her. She was standing in front of the jury. Confident, secure, calm. It was her opening statement, and she didn't waver.

"Hey," Zach said, interrupting her thoughts.

"Hi. What have you been up to?"

"Working on trial logistics. But we aren't cutting any corners. You will be safe."

"You know you can't make guarantees like that, Zach."

"I'm not just saying that to try to comfort you. I'm basing my opinion on the facts of the plan. I have experience in this area. I used to work in a private security firm for five years after college. It gave me a good background to apply for the FBI. So I have experience with event planning. Although I wasn't the one on the ground when I worked in the private sector. I was just the planner."

"That's interesting. Why did you leave that type of work?"

"I felt like I had pushed myself and learned everything that I could. I was starting to lose interest and wanted a new challenge. But I'm glad I didn't just apply to the FBI right out of college. Those years of work experience really helped me mature and gain skills that I found very valuable when I was at Quantico."

"I did just the opposite. My senior year of college I was busy preparing law school applications. I knew I wanted to be a lawyer and didn't waste any time. But there were quite a few people in my class who had other careers before going to law school. Or they had just taken a couple of years off to gain some other type of experience. Given my background, I felt more secure going directly into school. It wasn't like I had anyone to take care of me if something went wrong, so I took the safest course and went straight through."

"There's no right or wrong path when it comes to careers. Everyone has to choose what is best for them. I wasn't totally sure when I graduated if I wanted to go to the FBI, but after I experienced the private sector, it made the decision easier."

"A lot more lucrative in the private sector, though," she noted. "I know that well. I turned down a couple of offers to work at large Miami law firms. You wouldn't believe what they're willing to pay first-year associates at those big firms."

"But I'm guessing your heart wasn't in it?"

"No, not at all. I've held on to the dream of being a prosecutor for many years. It's not all about the money for me. It's about making a difference in people's lives. I'm not a fancy person. I don't need possessions to be happy. I've lived my whole life with so little. I don't think I'd be able to even appreciate that type of life-style." She paused. "And, yes, I do realize that my past has totally shaped pretty much every part of who I am today."

"There's nothing wrong with that. And I can relate to your decision-making process. I wanted a challenge at the FBI, but I also wanted to feel like I was work-ing on a team for a larger goal. Something bigger than myself. I've always enjoyed team sports and activities. So I thought it was a good fit for me."

"I guess at the end of the day, we both like helping people."

"And that's a good thing." He smiled. "What can I do to help you?"

She let out a big breath and pushed her hair back out of her eyes. "I am trying to stay positive, but I'm strug-gling. I know I've told you before, but without Denise's testimony, this is going to be nearly impossible. There's no other way to put it."

He reached out and touched her arm. "Think of it as a challenge. Yeah, you may have to stretch outside the box, but a jury can sense the truth. You have that on your side. That's the thing that matters most."

She shook her head. "But I've got to get to guilty beyond a reasonable doubt. That's no easy feat even with the best cases, with strong evidence and eyewitness testimony. I have neither of those things here. I know the defense is going to ask for a directed verdict when I finish my case."

"You've got enough to get past that stage. Don't you?"

She laughed. "See, now even you're wondering if this is going to be a weak case."

"I've got faith in you."

He was just being nice because he had no idea what her abilities were. "You haven't seen me in the courtroom. I could be a bad speaker."

"Nah. I can tell that you'll be good. Want to practice your opening statement? I can play juror."

"No. Practicing in front of you would just make me more nervous. All I can do is get back to it and make sure I have everything organized the best I can."

"If you change your mind, I'm here. Whatever you need, just ask. This is a team effort to make sure we get through this."

Jessica appreciated having Zach on her side. He was proving to be a source of strength and friendship for her. She wasn't used to letting someone into her life, but Zach was different.

She could only hope and pray that they would get through the trial and that she'd come out safely.

FIVE

Jessica had worked nonstop over the weekend preparing for the trial. And now it was Monday morning, and she felt as if she was going to be sick. She'd never really faced nerves in law school when she'd done the mock trial competitions. But right now she was having a serious case of jitters.

This wasn't just a random case. No, it was the prosecution of one of the most high-profile criminals in Miami. As her stomach churned, she took a few deep breaths to try to steady herself.

There was a loud knock on her bedroom door.

"Jessica, it's Zach. Are you ready?"

She didn't want Zach to see her sweat. *Lord, please give me the strength and wisdom to get through this first day of trial.* "I'll be right out."

Doing one last check in the mirror she was satisfied that her black suit paired with a gray blouse would be classic and understated for court. She wanted the jury to focus on the facts, not on her wardrobe choices.

She opened the door and walked down the stairs to

find Zach pacing around the kitchen. It was good to see that she wasn't the only one who was nervous.

"Hey," she said.

Zach stopped pacing and turned to her. "You look courtroom ready."

"Thanks. I'm anxious to get it started."

"Let's head out. Our security detail is waiting outside."

Hearing those words come out of his mouth made her stomach tighten even more. When he opened the front door and she walked out, she saw that "escort" was an understatement. It looked like a presidential motorcade. Five dark SUVs were on the street and lined up in front of the safe house.

"This is all for me?" she asked.

He guided her down the steps and toward the waiting vehicles. "Yes, I told you that we weren't taking any chances. We're getting you into that courthouse safely so you can focus on doing your part—which is to prosecute Simon Hernandez. I don't want you to be preoccupied or worried at all about the security side of things."

She watched as a few cars pulled out in front of theirs and the others followed behind. "Uh, Zach, don't you think this is going to draw way too much attention to the safe house? Isn't the point to be inconspicuous? This is anything but."

"Actually, yeah, I was going to tell you about that. We're going to be moving you to another location after we leave court today. Just being cautious. The FBI has plenty of options for safe houses, so it won't be an issue.

Your stuff will be packed up and will be waiting for you at the new location."

"All right. Sounds like a plan." She wasn't in a chatty mood, so she mainly kept quiet on the ride into downtown Miami.

The number of police vehicles around the courthouse was staggering. There was so much law enforcement presence that she was starting to believe Zach when he'd said nothing would happen to her.

"Here we are," Zach said. He pulled the SUV right up in front of the courthouse. "This is door-to-door service. I'll come around and help you out of the vehicle. Then you'll be flanked by me plus a few other FBI agents. No risks. No sudden moves. Just walk like you normally would. Got it?"

"Yes." What else could she say? That she was so nervous she was worried about getting sick right then and there? But it wasn't from the fear that someone was going to try to hurt her. No, it was whether she was going to be able to perform today when it really mattered. When she stood up for her opening statement and had to face the jury.

Taking a few more deep breaths, she told herself that it was going to be okay. And she reminded herself that she wasn't alone. She had God with her, which was even more important than the law enforcement presence.

Zach gently took her arm and guided her up the courthouse steps toward the door. Since he'd found out about her past, she'd noticed that he was very careful in how he touched her. The fact that it mattered so much to him meant a lot to her.

Once inside, she let out a breath. The first step was accomplished. Now they needed to get through the security line. There were no exceptions even for lawyers or law enforcement, and that was fine with her.

She set her bag down on the X-ray belt and showed her bar card, which allowed her to bring in her laptop and her phone.

"Are we headed directly to the courtroom?" she asked Zach.

"Yes. We will let you get settled in and ready to go."

The sooner she could get at counsel's table and get into the prosecutor zone, the better. There was too much commotion going on around her right now to get her head in the game.

One of the FBI agents opened the courtroom door, and Zach escorted her in. No one was allowed inside yet except for the attorneys and court staff, which instantly calmed her nerves.

Jessica went to work getting set up with her computer and files. Her paralegal was already there with the trial exhibits that she would use. Everything was in place and was proceeding just like any other case.

As people started to walk into the courtroom, her heartbeat pounded, and the calm she had been experiencing was instantly replaced with more jitters. All eyes were on her; she couldn't afford a misstep. That wasn't the way she'd planned to start her legal career. She didn't want to be the rookie prosecutor who fell flat on her face.

Members of the media filed in and sat in the reserved seating. She turned and eyed the reporters, who were like vultures circling their prey. Ready to bust open a big story or tweet out breaking news from the courtroom.

Lord, please give me the strength to do this. All she could do now was wait for the trial to begin.

Zach clenched and unclenched his fists as he assessed everyone who entered the courtroom. This wasn't just a regular assignment for him. Jessica had been through so much. She deserved someone who would look out for her, and he was the man for the job. Zach realized that he didn't just want to protect Jessica. He wanted to spend time with her on a personal level. He couldn't deny that he was starting to care for her.

Since this was the most high-profile trial in the area right now, the courtroom was going to be packed. Members of the general public had lined up starting hours ago to try to get one of the limited seats. This was a large courtroom, and he tried to make sure he looked at every single person to size them up as a potential threat. He looked down at his watch. The judge should be coming in any minute.

Looking toward the back right side of the courtroom, Zach was surprised to see Luke Hernandez. Despite everything he'd said at the safe house, now here was Luke openly flaunting his support for his brother by showing up at the trial. *Unbelievable.* It made Zach sick. Luke shouldn't be able to play both sides. He was an officer of the law and was supposed to take that responsibility seriously.

Zach refused to let the man's presence rattle him.

He had bigger concerns right now. So he took a seat in the first row behind where the lawyers sat. This gave him the best position to protect Jessica. Other agents were stationed throughout the courtroom to get a better vantage point of the entire scene in front of them. He felt good about the security presence, but he knew better than to let down his guard.

"All rise," the bailiff said.

Zach's attention was snapped back to the front as Judge Pamela Walker strode into the courtroom. The judge was in her mid-fifties and had a reputation for being tough on crime. But presiding over the trial of a member of the Hernandez family was another matter.

"You may be seated," Judge Walker said.

Zach looked over at the defense table. Simon Hernandez wore a dark designer suit that had probably cost a small fortune. His attorney, Mateo Tyson, was also similarly dressed and wore an ostentatious gold watch on his left wrist that couldn't be missed. Defending guys like Hernandez was a lucrative enterprise.

"Before we get started today, I want to set some ground rules," Judge Walker said. She took off her glasses, and her blue eyes were serious as she looked at the courtroom. "I realize that this is a case that is garnering a lot of attention from the community and the news media. We have a packed courtroom today, and I suspect it will be this way through the duration of the trial. But I want to make myself abundantly clear at the outset. I will absolutely not have any disruptions in my courtroom. I have a zero-tolerance policy. One misstep and you will be thrown out of court and held in contempt." She paused. "Hopefully, I have made myself clear. Counselors, are there any issues we need to take up before we start jury selection?"

Jessica stood up. "No, Your Honor. Nothing from the state."

"Or defense," Mateo said.

"Let's proceed, then," Judge Walker said.

Zach watched on closely for the next two hours as they went through the voir dire process and picked a jury. He knew that the next step was opening statements, and that's when the real action would begin.

"Is the state ready to go?" Judge Walker asked.

"Yes, Your Honor." Jessica stood up and started to walk to the podium.

He found himself waiting in anticipation for Jessica to speak. As he looked to the row behind him to his left, something caught his eye. A flash of metal from one of the female members of the media sitting in the front row of their designated section.

Acting purely on instinct, he yelled out, "Gun!"

He leaped over the small partition separating the counsel's area from the public and tackled Jessica to the ground, protecting her with his own body. He looked up as he continued to shield Jessica from any threats.

One of the bailiffs started running toward the woman.

Shrieks filled the courtroom, but the FBI agents were swarming around and had the situation under control as most people were sitting confused as to what had just happened. "Are you okay?" he asked Jessica.

Her breathing was heavy as she looked up at him with wide eyes. "I think so."

He looked back and saw that the woman was in custody, surrounded by police and FBI agents. She had her hands up in the air, and there was no gun in sight. Where was the gun? He knew he'd seen it.

"What just happened?" Jessica asked.

"She had a gun. I reacted based upon that." He paused and started to second-guess himself. "Or I thought I saw a gun."

"What was it, then?" she asked.

"I'm not sure. It looks like she's talking to them now." He really thought he had seen the weapon. He'd been certain of it. If there was no gun, then he had just made a huge mistake. One that a seasoned FBI agent wouldn't have made. This was going to be bad.

He pulled Jessica up off the ground and looked over at Simon Hernandez, who just stood there and gave him a smile. There was no doubt in Zach's mind that the Hernandez family would be gloating over his likely misstep.

The reporter yelled out. "I don't have a gun. It was just my compact." She held up her metal compact, showing it to the FBI agent right beside her and showing it off for the entire courtroom to see. A loud gasp sounded throughout the room. Just when he thought it couldn't get any worse. Had he really mistaken that metallic-looking makeup compact for a gun? Talk about amateur hour.

The judge banged the gavel loudly. "There will be order in this court."

Zach wanted to go hide in a corner somewhere.

The judge cleared her throat. "Given the highly unusual circumstances, we're going to take an extended recess. We'll resume the trial first thing in the morning so the situation here can be fully sorted out." The judge glared directly at him, and he felt as if he were back in elementary school being scolded by a teacher.

Brodie walked over to him. "We've got a new safe house ready for Jessica. And once we get back there, you and I need to have a talk."

Jessica sat at the new location in a state of shock. She'd asked for a little time alone to try to pull herself together. She couldn't believe that Zach had mistaken a makeup compact for a gun. And while she said she needed time alone, what she was really trying to do was give him some privacy to talk to Brodie.

She was worried what the repercussions would be for him. Yeah, he'd made a mistake, but she'd much rather he be overly aggressive than too complacent. The entire experience was surreal. One minute she'd been getting ready to give the most important opening statement of her life, and the next she was being tackled to the ground.

How would the trial be impacted by all of this? Would they just go back to business as usual tomorrow? And what would happen to Zach? He'd done what he thought was best to protect her, and she was going to fight for him.

She planned on getting some answers as she walked into the kitchen and found Zach and Brodie at the table.

"Hey, guys," she said as she took a seat.

"How are you feeling?" Brodie asked.

"I'm fine. I was a little rattled, but once all the facts came out, I realized that there was nothing to be worried about." She eyed Zach warily. "And what's going on here?"

"I take full responsibility for my mistake," Zach said. "I owe you an apology."

"Apology for what? You did what you thought was best under the circumstances."

"I reacted quickly based on instincts, but in this case they were completely wrong."

"What is the reporter saying?"

"That she was innocently pulling out her makeup compact from her purse," Brodie said. He frowned and looked at her. "This doesn't make the FBI look so good."

The next question was even more important to her. "Where does this leave us with the trial?"

"We will go back to court tomorrow and resume where we left off—you'll do your opening statement, and we'll proceed from there. I'm going to have a private meeting with the judge first thing in the morning to try to smooth things over with her. The last thing I want is for her to think that I was being reckless—it was just the opposite."

"Well, you would think that the judge would be appreciative of how alert you were." Her heart hurt for Zach. This was going to be something he wasn't going to just get over in a few hours. This could have a lasting impact on him.

Brodie looked at her. "Are you okay to go back in the morning and resume the trial?"

"Are you kidding me?" she asked. "Of course I want to continue. We can't let them think that this will in any way impact the resolve of the prosecutor's office. Simon Hernandez must face a jury for his crimes, and I intend to be the person prosecuting him." If anything, these latest events made her more determined to push forward strongly. Yes, she knew they had to keep their guard up, but she refused to let fear dictate how she would live her life.

"I'm going to get out of here. You have extra security outside and, of course, Zach. So you will be secure," Brodie said.

"Thank you."

Brodie left, and now it was just her and Zach inside the safe house.

"You have a lot you want to say," Zach said.

"You're right. I don't want you to beat yourself up over this. No one is perfect. I imagine that other FBI agents in your position would have acted the same way. You were just doing your job."

He shook his head. "That was a world-class error, Jessica. And that's why we need to talk."

"All right." She had an idea of where this was going, and she already didn't like it. But she was going to hear him out.

"I've talked this over with Brodie, and he agrees. If you would prefer to have another FBI agent step in and replace me, then we will make that happen. As soon as tomorrow morning, in fact. Brodie has a couple of guys lined up."

She shook her head. "No way. Would you expect me to just give up on you right now over one misstep?"

"I wouldn't blame you one bit for wanting another agent on your security detail. I promise you it won't hurt my feelings. I have to be objective about this. My lack of experience showed in that courtroom. I can't deny that fact, and you shouldn't, either. No matter how nice you want to be about everything that happened today."

Now she was getting worked up. "Don't do this, Zach. You're selling yourself short. We all make mistakes. And I am glad you acted today, because what if that had been a gun? If you hadn't reacted the way you did, I would definitely be dead. So if it means that sometimes we're wrong in an effort to keep ourselves safe, that's something I can more than live with."

"Are you certain about this? Because I'm fully prepared to walk away."

"You better not. You made a commitment to me, and you are going to stick it out. This is no time to run away. And you can tell the FBI that you are the only agent I will accept working with me."

"I can't believe you've placed so much trust in me."

"Honestly, I can't, either, but it feels right. And I do trust you—with my life. Don't ever forget that." She reached out and touched his hand. Finding contentment in the connection between the two of them. And maybe even a longing for something more. "You've been there for me each step of the way. So I'm here for you right now. I know this is tough for you, but it's all part of becoming a better agent."

He squeezed her hand. "I really appreciate you saying that."

"And who knows? What if I totally lose it during my opening statement tomorrow?"

He smiled. "Then we'd be even, I guess. But I know that won't happen. You've got this, Jessica. I can tell by the look in your eyes."

"Thanks. It's almost like I get a do-over. I was so nervous today. I have a feeling I won't be nearly as nervous tomorrow. So at the end of the day, maybe it all worked out for the best."

"I'm here for you. I wouldn't want to have it any other way, and you need to know that."

"Thank you." She fought back the tears that were threatening to fill her eyes. Zach was a good guy. She'd experienced so much pain in her life. But letting Zach in wasn't bringing her hurt—just the opposite. He was trying his best to protect her and keep her safe. She wasn't used to anyone standing up for her. It was a job she had done by herself all her life, but having him by her side now felt right. And she didn't want to let him go.

His phone rang, and she watched as he took it out of his jacket and answered. She listened to the one-sided conversation but couldn't put together exactly what was going on. She waited for him to finish the call and then looked up at him as he frowned deeply.

"What's wrong?"

"That was Brodie. He just got a call from the court."

"And?" She wondered what they'd have to say about all of this.

"Judge Walker is unhappy about the entire situation. She has agreed to meet me in the morning. Brodie says she isn't convinced that there wasn't some sort of purposeful action on my part to delay things. That doesn't make any sense to me, but I'll have to convince her that I was just doing what I thought was best in the moment. All I can do is tell the truth. Brodie mentioned that by the end of the conversation she seemed more receptive." He let out a breath. "She expects the parties to be back in the courtroom at nine a.m. tomorrow."

"That reminds me. I need to talk to Ian and check in with him."

"Okay, but since I feel like we have a totally open line of communication, I need to say something else."

"All right. What's on your mind?"

"I don't trust Ian. He clearly has strong ambitions. I think he's reaping all the benefits of this trial without having to actually put himself on the line." Zach stood up and started pacing around the kitchen. "It bothers me that he's using you like that."

She stood and walked over to Zach. "But I don't see it like that at all. This is an opportunity of a lifetime. He could take it away and do it himself or reassign it to a senior prosecutor. But he didn't do that. He's given me the chance to prove myself as a first-year lawyer. That's something I can't turn away from."

"Even if it's your life on the line?"

She smiled. "I have the best security team in the world. Even with all the threats, I'm perfectly safe. As long as you and your guys keep doing your job, then it will be fine."

"I appreciate your faith in us especially after what happened today."

"I don't want you to think another thought about that. I need you fully back and engaged tomorrow for the resumption of trial."

"And you need to get some rest. You've got a big day tomorrow."

"Don't worry. I'm ready. It will take a lot more than this to stop me from doing my job." And she meant every word.

SIX

Much to her surprise, Jessica woke up the next morning having slept better than she had in days. Last night, she'd been forthright with Zach. She did appreciate the FBI team. They were top-notch, and seeing them in action gave her a level of comfort. Zach's overreaction might not have been justified, but she appreciated his effort and attention to the threats. She had meant it when she had said that she didn't want anyone else in charge of her security.

And this afternoon as she sat at the counsel's table readying herself for her opening statement, she maintained her focus. It occurred to her as she gripped a red pen tightly in her hand that she was angry. The Hernandez family thought they could bully her into submission, but that wasn't how she operated. No, she was going to face down Simon and try her best to get a conviction—even against all the obstacles that had piled up in her way.

"The floor is yours for opening statements, Ms. Hughes," Judge Walker said.

Because of her reputation of being tough on criminals, Jessica felt she had an ally in Judge Walker. But the judge would still be fair in her rulings even if Hernandez was guilty.

She looked back and saw that Zach was in the front row. He gave her a slight nod. She had this.

"Thank you, Your Honor. And good afternoon, ladies and gentlemen of the jury." Much to her surprise, the defense hadn't moved for a new jury after yesterday's events, but the judge had ordered it. So now with the new jury they had spent the morning picking, they were ready to go.

"The evidence will show that the defendant, Mr. Simon Hernandez, is guilty of multiple criminal counts of money laundering under the federal and state laws. Let me unpack that just a little bit for you. The first count of money laundering is that the defendant, Simon Hernandez, engaged in financial transactions, involving the proceeds of crimes, in order to conceal the fact of the underlying criminal activity. The second count of money laundering is that Mr. Hernandez engaged in financial transactions involving criminal proceeds in order to evade taxes on the income produced by his criminal activity. And the final count alleges that Mr. Hernandez transported funds generated by criminal activities into and out of the United States in order to promote his criminal activities."

She made direct eye contact with each and every juror as she walked them through the charges in more detail, giving them a preview of what was to come. It wasn't her style to be inflammatory or over-the-top. Financial crimes were difficult to simplify and even more difficult to discuss in a manner that didn't put the jury to sleep. This case didn't have the purely emotional appeal a murder case would. But the jury stayed with her during the forty-five-minute opening statement.

When she sat down, she felt she'd done the best job she could. Now it was time to watch Mateo in action. It was guaranteed to be a show. Mateo was known as being a highly flamboyant and animated defense attorney.

"I'm Mateo Tyson. I represent Mr. Hernandez. I won't take as much time today as Ms. Hughes took, and the reason behind that is actually pretty simple. The state has the burden of proof in this case. And the state simply won't be able to produce a shred of credible evidence tying Mr. Hernandez to any of these alleged crimes. Regardless of all of the smoke and mirrors from Ms. Hughes, at the end of the trial you will have to ask yourself if the state has proven their case beyond a reasonable doubt. And I am confident that once all the evidence is presented, my client will be acquitted."

Mateo went on and covered a few factual points, but, true to his word, his opening was about half as long as hers and presented with the ease and technique of someone who'd been lawyering for twenty-five years. She knew she had the harder job. Especially since they'd killed off her star witness. But unfortunately she couldn't say that. The reason for Denise's unavailability for trial was prohibited from being discussed because it had been determined by the judge to be unduly prejudicial to the jury. Of course, if the jury heard that the star witness had been murdered just days ago, it would impact their thinking. Which is why the judge barred the introduction of that evidence. So Jessica was stuck with what she had. Which admittedly wasn't much.

"Call your first witness, Ms. Hughes."

The rest of the afternoon progressed with Jessica laying out her case the best way she could. But she could see the skepticism apparent on the faces of a few of the jurors. By the time the judge decided to recess, Jessica was ready to call it a day.

She made the mistake of looking over at Simon, and he grinned at her. The man was certainly trying to get into her head. But she wouldn't succumb to his games—whether they were mental or physical threats.

"Good job," Zach said into her ear.

She turned to face him. "Thank you."

"Let's get you out of here."

"That would be great." She needed to decompress after a full day in court.

By the time they got back to the safe house, she was ravenous and glad that one of the agents had dinner brought in quickly.

As she sat across the table from Zach, she wanted to know his thoughts. "I have to ask—how do you think it went today? And before you answer, you don't have to be diplomatic. You won't hurt my feelings. I want your honest opinion."

He nodded. "Don't worry. I think you'll find out soon enough that I'm a straight shooter. Maybe to a fault. I think your performance was strong. You were in command of the evidence and had a strong presence in front of the jury. But I think there are some big evidentiary holes that we both knew would be a problem."

"You're right. I noticed a few jurors seemed particularly skeptical about some of what I presented and the connections I was trying to make."

"You can only do what you can with what you have. As long as you do your best, then that's all anyone can ask for."

She rubbed her temples. "And if Simon walks, then what?"

"There's always the investigation into Ana. She's even dirtier than Simon."

"I don't know if the state would want to immediately take her on if Simon is acquitted."

"Nothing you can do about that, either. All you can do is focus on what is in your ability to control."

"I hear you. But it's easier said than done." Worrying about things that were out of her control was one of her weak points.

"Did you happen to see who was sitting in the back row of the courtroom?"

"Luke Hernandez?"

"Yes. And he was there yesterday, too."

Zach just wouldn't give up on his pursuit of Luke. "Are we back to that again?"

"Yes. Don't you think it's strange? Why would he be coming to his brother's trial if not to show support?"

She leaned forward. "Maybe he wants to see his brother be held responsible for his crimes. Have you even considered that?"

He crossed his arms. "I like my theory better."

"But Luke is not our problem. Even if he wanted to be there because his brother was on trial, I don't think that's a crime."

"It's just the optics of the entire thing. The message that it sends that a member of the Miami police department would be in any way supporting the defense."

"I think you should focus your time elsewhere."

"I know I won't be able to convince you without evidence directly tying Luke back to the family. Regardless of his exact intentions, I don't trust him."

After sitting through three days of trial, Zach was anxious to know what verdict the jury had reached. While Jessica had done an admirable job, he was worried that the jurors would find more than enough reasonable doubt. But Jessica didn't really seem fazed by much—whether it was an attack on her life or the possibility of an acquittal. She stayed strong and continued to impress him by the minute. He admired her tenacity and ability to push through in the face of adversity.

As the jurors were led back into the courtroom, he took a few deep breaths. His focus still remained on Jessica's security.

"Have you reached a verdict?" Judge Walker asked the foreperson.

The foreperson stood. "Yes, Your Honor. We have."

Zach watched on with anticipation as the verdict was handed to the judge to review and then back to the foreperson. He looked over at Jessica, who sat devoid of any expression. His stomach tightened as he felt certain he knew what words were going to come out of the foreperson's mouth.

"On the first count of money laundering, we the jury find Simon Hernandez not guilty."

The foreperson kept on reading, finding Simon not guilty on all three counts. The courtroom crowd started talking, which drew consternation from the judge.

After the judge dismissed the jury and court was officially out of session, Zach walked up to Jessica, who was gathering her things at counsel's table.

"I'm going to have to take a few questions from the media. Ian said I would need to do that regardless of the outcome." She put her laptop bag over her shoulder. "I have to act like this is just business as usual."

"I'm sorry about that. I'll be right beside you, though." And he meant it. He was going to stick close to Jessica, not only for her own security but also for the moral support. Even though they were both expecting a not-guilty verdict, it was still tough to have to manage the aftermath. He didn't envy her position one bit. And he wasn't going to take any chances with her safety. Even though the trial was over, an official threat assessment still needed to take place.

She looked up at him. "The media hounds will be right outside the courthouse wanting to get statements and ask questions."

"Understood. Better for you to just get this over with, then."

He guided her out the courtroom doors and down the long corridor to the front exit of the building. They still had their FBI team working the perimeter and as-

sisting him with Jessica's security. He felt pretty sure
that between all the agents, she'd be secure in speaking with the media.

"Here goes nothing." She stepped out of the building
onto the courthouse steps, where there was a crowd of
reporters waiting for her.

He was on high alert as he scoped out all the faces.
The likelihood of something happening right after the
acquittal would be low given that the Hernandez family was probably too focused on celebrating. But he
was still cautious as he surveyed the crowd. The flash-
ing lights from the photographers drove him crazy, but
there was nothing he could do about it.

"Ms. Hughes," one female reporter yelled out. "What
do you think about the jury's verdict?"

He looked on and prepared himself for the worst,
but Jessica kept her composure and made direct eye
contact with the reporter. "I respect the jury's decision
and appreciate them taking time out of their schedules
to do their civic duty."

"But you can't feel good about this?" the reporter
followed up.

"I'm obviously disappointed, but that's the nature
of litigation and our criminal justice system. It's much
harder for the prosecution to prove beyond a reasonable
doubt. We have those checks and balances in the system
for a reason, and I also respect that. At the end of the
day, of course, my hope was for a guilty verdict on all
three counts, but that didn't happen. We will move on
from this and continue with our business at the prosecutor's office."

A male reporter stepped forward. "How do you answer criticism that you never should've been the one trying this case to begin with since you just graduated law school and haven't even been at the prosecutor's office for a full year?"

Ugh. Talk about a low blow. Zach had confidence that Jessica wouldn't be so easily rattled by comments about her level of experience.

She smoothed down her suit jacket and straightened her shoulders, standing tall. "While you are correct about me being a fairly new lawyer, I worked on this case for months under a very seasoned lawyer who, because of health reasons, had to step aside. I was fully prepared, and I did the best I could do with the evidence I had."

The male reporter took a step forward. "And why was your case so weak?"

"Our case wasn't as strong as we would've liked, but a lot of that was beyond our control."

"Why didn't you have better evidence, though?" another reporter chimed in.

"We had an eyewitness that unfortunately was murdered before the trial."

A loud set of gasps rippled throughout the crowd. Zach was surprised, too. He hadn't expected Jessica to put that out there like that. But she acted as if she knew exactly what she was doing.

"What do you mean?" the reporter asked.

"Why didn't we hear about this?" another reporter yelled.

The media circus had just gone from one ring to

three. He stayed close to Jessica, keeping his eyes on the crowd.

"I can explain. You never heard about our witness because we were subject to a gag order on this topic. But now that the case is over, I can speak freely."

"Who was this person?"

"Her name was Denise Landers, and she worked for the Hernandez family, handling their accounting. Suspiciously, right before trial, our star witness was murdered. I don't think I have to spell it out for any of you. So that obviously impacted our case."

"What would Ms. Landers have testified to?"

"As an accountant for Simon Hernandez, she had personal knowledge of facts that would have substantiated all aspects of the case."

The reporters kept yelling out questions, but Jessica was done. "Thank you, everyone." She nodded toward Zach, and he took her by the arm and escorted her down the steps to where the SUV was waiting for them.

Once in the safety of his SUV, he looked over at her. "You're putting on a very brave face, but I know you have to be upset."

She nodded. "I am, but this outcome wasn't unexpected."

"You threw me a curveball back there. I had no idea you were going to bring up Denise's murder to the media."

"I had Ian's approval to do so once the verdict was issued. And when they went in for the kill, I figured I would give them something to think about. If nothing else, it certainly raises the possibility of Simon's guilt at least with the public and in the media. It's a very small victory, but it's something."

"We're regrouping at the safe house to talk about next steps."

"Will I be able to go back to my normal life now? I miss Tiger so much and my simple apartment with my things. I may not have a lot, but at least what I have is mine."

"That's one of the things we're going to have to talk about. Ian is coming over, as well. I wanted to get input from him on how to move forward."

"Because if I go after Ana, you think it will still be dangerous for me."

"There's no doubt in my mind."

"We still don't know if Ian is going to be on board with another prosecution of the Hernandez family right now."

"Which is why we need to talk about it."

"Don't get me wrong. I want to make a case against her, but I need to make sure it's a stronger one than this was. And I'm also not looking forward to continuing my life on lockdown. I miss Tiger. I miss my quiet life."

He knew what she wanted to hear, but he would only tell her the truth. "Your life may never be so quiet again."

She groaned.

"We can talk about all of this at the meeting. Just try to relax on the rest of the way over."

Relax, she thought. That would be a nice concept, but the word wasn't part of her vocabulary. As she looked into the eyes of her boss as they all gathered around the large dining room table at the safe house, the last thing she was feeling was relaxed.

Brodie, Zach and Ian all had a lot of ideas, and she wanted to make sure her voice was also heard. She had to be careful, though, because at the end of the day, Ian was still her superior and she wasn't in a position to make demands on him about her assignments.

"Before we really jump into moving forward, I just wanted to say something at the outset," Ian said. "Jessica, you took on a very tough assignment and really put on the strongest case you could. The entire office is proud of your efforts."

"Thank you, Ian. That means a lot to me." And it did. The affirmation felt good after the disappointing results.

"It's important that you don't take this verdict personally. We all knew it was an uphill battle after Denise's murder. And frankly, it would've been a tough case even if Denise had been alive to testify against Simon."

"I understand. We have to do the best we can with the evidence we have."

"Exactly. But I realize we're gathered here tonight to talk about next steps," Ian said.

"Right," Zach said. "The FBI is currently conducting a threat assessment to determine how best to proceed with regard to Jessica's security."

"And that is a top priority for me," Ian said. "What are you guys thinking right now? I know you're doing a formal analysis, but this will impact my thinking on what happens next regarding the Hernandez family."

Brodie leaned forward. "I don't think anyone at the bureau thinks that Jessica is totally in the clear. This family holds a grudge. Yeah, they won this battle, but there's a larger war out there."

"Do you really think they'd be so blatant as to go after Jessica again? Especially after all that has happened?" Ian asked.

"I do," Zach responded. "But that actually dovetails into something else I know we all wanted to talk about—building a case against Ana."

"Do you have a plan?" Ian asked.

"If we really want to go after Ana, then we have to understand that Jessica will still be in danger. Assuming everyone wants to move forward, I'll continue to provide for her personal security. And we'll work this case together."

"That's an interesting game plan. Given Jessica's knowledge regarding the Hernandez family, it only makes sense that she'd continue as the prosecutor on any follow-up litigation. What's the FBI's position on Ana's investigation?" Ian asked.

"We've got a lot of action going on," Brodie said. "Ana's knee-deep into the same things as her brother. Plus we believe with a bit more digging we're going to get the hard evidence to tie her to drug trafficking. Not low-level distribution-type stuff, but major movement of product. We have a confidential informant that is extremely close to bringing us something that could make the strongest case possible against Ana."

"If we go down this path, I would want this to be a highly collaborative effort between our office and the

FBI. And I will not assign Jessica this case if the FBI decides to pull her security. It's just too risky. So that's an absolute nonnegotiable."

"I doubt that's going to happen," Brodie said. "I don't think we'd consider doing that given the level of danger. The issue will more likely be how much security is assigned to her."

"I don't need a full security team, guys. If Zach and I are going to be working on the Ana investigation together, he's totally able to handle anything that could come up."

Ian looked at her. "So I take it, Jessica, that you really want to move forward and continue to work on matters related to the Hernandez family?"

"Absolutely." She knew what she was getting into, but she believed so strongly that this family had to be stopped.

"Then assuming you have FBI security in place and are working jointly with them to build a case against Ana, I will approve it."

"Thank you, Ian." She felt a resurgence of excitement. She might have lost against Simon, but there was still another fight to be had. And she intended to take down the Hernandez family once and for all.

SEVEN

Zach organized his paper files and laptop on the dining room table of the safe house. Much to his relief, he'd been given the go-ahead by the higher-ups to stay with Jessica and continue to provide for her security. And even better, he had the big green light to push forward on the investigation of Ana Hernandez. He felt as a team, he and Jessica could put together a rock-solid case.

Jessica also seemed excited about the prospect of working with him. And that made him happy. They were different in many ways, but they both had the same passionate drive.

Jessica walked into the room with her laptop in her hands. "I'm ready to work," she said.

"Great—me, too." Zach adjusted the screen on his computer.

He looked over at Jessica as she took a seat. Her blond hair was hanging loose down her shoulders this afternoon. Often he found himself looking at her not as part of his security detail, but as a woman he cared for. He could actually see her in his life once this case was over. Because the more he got to know Jessica, the more he liked her. And he already had a tremendous amount of respect for her after only a short time. Although his feelings for her went beyond respect.

"Where do you want to start?" she asked.

"From the ground up. Everything we each know about Ana Hernandez. You want to kick us off?"

"Sure." She consulted her notes on her laptop. "Ana is thirty years old. Single and maintains at least two known residences. One near her family's home in Coral Springs and another on South Beach. She owns a dry cleaning business and a deli-style restaurant. My latest research indicates that she also just put an offer in on another piece of real estate. I don't know what plans she has for that."

"Interesting. What have you uncovered on her ties to illegal activities?"

Jessica cocked her head to the side. "She's not as bulletproof as her brother or father. I think if we drill down hard enough on the financials, we'll find at the very least enough evidence to substantiate a money laundering charge in conjunction with her businesses. But if we're going after her, I don't want to bring only money laundering charges like I did with Simon. I want the drug trafficking to be a part of it. That's what really makes this a bigger and better case."

"Well, if our FBI confidential informant comes through, then we might have the drug-trafficking angle against Ana. Our CI didn't have as much access to Simon, but he is close to Ana. We know for a fact that she's orchestrating some pretty complex drug-smuggling operations, but it's just a matter of gathering the evidence to prove it. Which is harder than it sounds since there's always different levels of middlemen that are involved to protect the family."

"Given all that's happened, you have to wonder if they're going to be a bit more cautious from here on out?"

"Or after the acquittal, they're even more confident and think that they're above the law and untouchable. They'll be emboldened to do whatever they want because they think a jury will never convict them."

"Let them get arrogant," she said. "That will only increase the likelihood that we'll catch a break. How much do you know about the CI?"

"He's built up credibility over the past few years working as a CI for the FBI. But he hasn't been in a position up until this point to bring in something major. It takes years working for the Hernandez family before you get to the level where you'd have access to the type of information that we need to build our case. But now they've put him in charge of negotiating with suppliers and that gives him access to information regarding the drug trafficking."

"And how long has he been working for Hernandez?"

"Fifteen years."

"And what makes someone like that turn?" she asked.

"It's different for each CI. Sometimes it's the hope that they can take their families and start over with brand-new lives in witness protection. But that's only reserved for the ones that bring in the most valuable evidence. For others, they get tired of the lifestyle or feel like they aren't treated fairly or compensated enough. I don't know yet what our guy's motivation is, and I'm not as concerned about that as I am about what he can actually bring us."

"I can imagine that a lot of guys make promises but then aren't able to follow through."

He nodded. "And, yeah, that's when things can go south quickly, especially if there's ever any doubt about the CI's allegiance to the family. Mick Hernandez has standing orders. Shoot first and worry later about whether it was the right thing to do. His iron-fist method of ruling ensures that most of the people that work for him wouldn't even consider turning against the family."

"Harsh but highly effective."

"You've seen it with how they've gone after you, Jessica."

"Yeah, I know. All of this makes me think our CI has to have a strong source of motivation for risking his life. I hope the FBI has a solid plan in place to protect him."

"Of course. We don't take this lightly. Everyone is fully involved and engaged."

"Okay. So back to our original topic of discussion. I've told you what I know. Now it's your turn. What information do you have on Ana that you can share?" she asked.

"The drug trafficking is where the bureau has focused their attention. We've gathered lots of intel—the issue is going to be connecting the dots and shoring up the evidence. We believe Ana is using her legitimate businesses as a cover to run drugs throughout the city. She's building a highly sophisticated transportation network, and there's been a lot of activity at the loading docks. Yes, she has legitimate business products coming in via ship transport, but we believe that's only part of the story and that drugs are coming into the country this way. And that the Hernandez family is trying to up its game to become a top player in the drug business."

"If they're doing so well with their other illegal efforts, then why even bother with the drug trafficking?" Jessica wondered.

"Because there's so much money to be had there. They're not going to leave that type of cash on the table. Yes, it means they have to shift up some of their business models, but it's clear to me that decision has been made. Granted, I've only been working this case a short time, but I've read every file I can get my hands on, and I'm constantly reviewing the intel reports."

"We had limited evidence on the drug business for Simon's case, but there wasn't anything concrete to put before the jury."

"Once you get in the drug business, it amplifies all your other work. I know Mick runs a casino business. Gambling and drugs go hand in hand," Zach explained.

"You might as well start looking into weapons trafficking, too."

"The FBI has, but so far nothing on that front. I think all of their effort right now is on taking over as the largest distributor in the city and beyond, for that matter."

"You can't run a large operation like that under the radar forever."

"Yeah. It's a matter of when, not if," he said. He hoped it would be sooner rather than later, but Jessica was right. This thing was going to get too big for Ana to hide in the shadows forever. "We were both thrown right into the middle of this thing. But now it seems like we've been working together on these cases forever."

"I know, right?" She smiled.

He felt his heart constrict for a moment as he once again realized how much he enjoyed spending time with Jessica. "Sometimes I feel like I've been in the FBI for much longer than I have, but then there are times I realize that I still have a lot to learn." He paused. "Even beyond my obvious misstep in court." He still was having a hard time moving past that.

"You should be proud of yourself, Zach. In my opinion, you've risen to the occasion in every way."

"Thank you for saying that. I could say the same thing about you and then some. You've really shown no fear, Jessica. It's one of the most amazing things I've ever seen. How you've faced down the Hernandez family even when you've been attacked and threatened."

"It's because I don't rely on myself for my strength, Zach. I rely on God."

"I really admire your faith. I like to think that I've grown a lot in my faith over the years, but you're showing me that I still have a ways to go."

"In what way?"

"You have a total reliance on God. Or at least it seems that way to me. I have trouble really letting go and letting God take control. Even when it's my strongest intention to do so, there are times I get off track and just start doing things my way."

"It's not easy, Zach. And my background made me

rely on Him because He was all I had. There was no other option. No parent or friend looking out for me. No person that I could confide in or trust. I knew so much hardship and pain that finding my faith literally meant the difference between life and death. I completely believe that with every part of me. But I'm far from perfect. I get stubborn and focus on doing things on my own, too. It's not just you."

He ran a hand through his hair. "I fully recognize that I'm self-sufficient and probably a bit too self-centered. But I'm working on it."

She shook her head. "You have a warped perception of yourself. Since I've met you, you've been totally selfless, not selfish." She reached out and grabbed on to his arm.

He couldn't help but be affected by her warm touch. Especially with the knowledge of her past and understanding what it took for her to be close to him like that.

"And I'm enjoying our partnership," she said. "Don't discount the fact that I can learn things from you, too."

He liked the sound of the partnership they had. "I can tell how passionate you are about your beliefs. If anything, that just makes me like you even more. I consider you a friend, Jessica." In his mind, though, he wanted more than friendship between them.

Later that night sitting in the living room, Jessica brought up a subject that had been weighing on her since their earlier conversation. "I want to meet the CI," she said, looking into Zach's eyes as she made her request.

"Jessica, that's not the smartest idea. We can't have him come here. There would be far too much exposure. And it's too dangerous to have you meet him elsewhere. If anyone saw you together, he would be as good as dead, and the target on your back would just get bigger. Our case would be severely impacted if we lose the CI. So it's just not something that's going to happen."

"If he could get to the safe house undetected, though..." Wasn't the FBI supposed to be good at that? Getting people places without others knowing? Operating under the radar?

"I'm sorry, Jess. You can debate me all you want, but this particular item is nonnegotiable."

She laughed. "So now I'm Jess?"

"Sorry. Guess you don't like that nickname?"

"The nickname doesn't bother me. It's the part about non-negotiation that does. Are you sure we can't come to a middle ground?"

"Not on this. And, anyway, even if you could win me over, this isn't my call since I'm not running the CI." He paused, and his eyes softened. "Tell me what you think meeting him will tell you that you can't get from the FBI side."

"I like to be able to validate a witness's credibility myself. Face-to-face. With the FBI involved, everything is sanitized."

"I don't want you to think the bureau is holding back information. Whatever we know, you now know. The only difference is a face-to-face meet is off the table at this point. Obviously, if you end up charging Ana and you move forward with the prosecution, then you'd be meeting with the CI just like any of your other witnesses to prepare him to testify."

"Yeah, but the entire analysis of the case may hinge on the CI's testimony. If I can't evaluate him myself, then that could lead to problems down the road."

"I see your perspective, but security concerns are going to trump the legal ones. That's just the way it is."

"What about a virtual meeting? Where I can at least see him and talk to him?"

"You are a tough one, Jess."

"There you go again." She couldn't help but smile. She actually enjoyed being called Jess. She'd never really had anyone call her that. Mainly because she didn't let people get close enough to her to allow for that type of familiarity. But with Zach she seemed to be breaking her normal rules. Instead of the nickname bothering her, it actually made her feel close to him in a way she'd never experienced before.

"I wasn't even thinking about an electronic meeting. I'm sure there are still risks with setting that up, but I'm willing to at least pitch the idea to Brodie and see what he thinks. The problem is that I don't know if there's anything that would make him want to take a risk in compromising our guy. Maybe once we pull him out and have him in protective custody if it comes to that."

Even though she wanted to interview the CI for herself, ultimately she knew that Zach was right. None of them could afford compromising the informant. And she definitely didn't want that on her conscience if something went wrong. "All right. I'm sympathetic to your point. And obviously the last thing I'd want to do is to risk the CI's life or well-being."

"Good. Sounds like we're in agreement then for the time being."

"Maybe not for long."

"Uh-oh," he said. "What else do you have for me?"

"I want to scope out some of Ana's businesses."

"Scope out?"

"Yeah, as in go there and see things for myself."

"You do realize that you're not an agent, or even a detective, right? You're the prosecutor."

She smiled. "Yes, I've very aware of my role, but I'm working with you. We're supposed to be a team. We need to see what's going on for ourselves. Especially the shipping operation and the transportation networks she has set up near the marina."

He cocked his head to the side. "You're really interested in stepping into danger, aren't you?"

"You said we were going to investigate. To be able to do so, we have to get out there—we can't stay shut up in here forever. I'm not saying that we should be reckless or take unnecessary risks, but we need to get a bit more aggressive in our investigation. Maybe we'll notice things out there which will lead us to investigate other facts or leads."

"You'll have to let me be the judge of how far to push the envelope. I'm a member of law enforcement, and you're a member of the bar. We aren't private investigators, so there are limits to what we can do. The last thing we would need is some sort of civil complaint filed by the Hernandez family against us."

"I know that."

The doorbell interrupted their conversation. Jessica looked over at Zach. "Were you expecting someone?"

"No, but it's possible it could be a team member with updates. Stay here while I check it out."

She waited patiently at the table, and before long she heard an additional male voice. Then Detective Will Lang entered the room.

"How are you doing, Jessica?" Will asked.

The detective had been kind to her from the start. "I'm okay. I'm assuming you have some sort of news for us?"

"Nothing groundbreaking, but we know that you two are working on the investigation into Ana Hernandez. The word on the street is that something is going to go down at some point as soon as this weekend."

"Like what?" Zach asked.

"That's the problem. I almost didn't even tell you this because the tip was so vague, but in the interest of sharing information between agencies, I thought I would. I didn't want you angry with me after the fact if something happened and you learned that I didn't share the intel. So that's why I'm here. Just trying to be fully transparent with you."

"No location, no subject matter, nothing?" Jessica asked. It was almost worse to hear this and not be able to really act on it.

"No, I'm sorry. This is just chatter our guys are picking up off the street. So could it just be rumor or innuendo? Sure. But something else could be going on."

All the more reason for them to be out there instead of locked up in the safe house. But she figured she would wait until Will left to continue that discussion with Zach.

"If you get any more intel, please let me know ASAP," Zach said.

"Of course. Anything else that the Miami PD can do for you?"

"Anyone on your team have their eye on Luke Hernandez?"

Will shook his head. "We don't investigate our own like that. Or at least not outside of internal affairs."

"What's your read on him?" Jessica asked.

"Personally, I think he's a good guy that's part of a bad family. But I know there are others who don't share my views. I can tell you that the majority sees it like I do. Luke has a stellar reputation on the force, and he's always the guy who lends a hand to others. He's the first to answer if you call him for anything. In my book, that goes a long way to someone's character."

"Or it goes to someone who knows how to keep up a strong cover."

Jessica shook her head. "Zach, you're barking up the wrong tree again."

Zach looked over at Will. "Back me up here, Will."

"It's your job to be suspicious of everyone. That's how you've been able to keep Jessica safe. So I wouldn't argue with your approach. We all have different roles to play here."

"I'd agree with that," Jessica said. "And my chief focus right now is on Ana Hernandez, not her brother Luke. And until some actual evidence turns up to convince me otherwise, then thinking about him is a waste of our time. We should be trying to get what we need to charge Ana."

"If there's anything else that comes up, I'll let you guys know," Will said.

Jessica nodded. "Thanks for coming over."

Zach walked Will out, and she could hear them talking in low tones. About what she didn't know, but she didn't like being in the dark. This was as much her investigation as it was the FBI's. Her office would be the one bringing charges against another member of the Hernandez family.

When Zach returned to the living room she was ready for some answers. "What were you discussing as Will left?"

"Just me trying to push him on that intel he gave us. I think he's holding back on us, and I don't know why."

"Why would he do that? He didn't even have to bring us the info to begin with."

"Well, he kinda did. At least this way he can say that he shared information. But I think he knows more than he was letting on."

She smiled. "Are you always this suspicious of everyone?"

"What do you mean?"

"You don't take anything at face value from anybody."

"You heard Will. It's my job to always be questioning. I learned that lesson the hard way at Quantico. We had this one simulation exercise, and I took a piece of information as it was given to me. I assumed the person who gave me the intel was forthright. And then I learned at the end of the exercise that he was a bad guy, and my actions would've gotten an innocent person killed. So the lesson that day for me was this—if you just go with the flow and blindly listen to what others say, that's how people end up getting killed."

A chill shot through her body as she listened to his words. "I guess I'm being a little narrow-minded. I live my life in a legal box that doesn't always get to see the ins and outs of the practical on-the-ground investigation."

His eyes widened. "Did you just concede a point, Counselor?"

"I guess I did. Whether you believe it or not, it's not always about winning the argument for me."

"I never said it was."

Her phone rang, and she looked down and saw it was an unidentified number. She'd been given a special burner phone by the FBI, and very few people had the number. "Hello," she said.

"Ms. Hughes," a male voice said.

"Yes. Who is this?"

"It's Mick Hernandez."

She mouthed who it was to Zach and put the phone on Speaker. "How did you get this number, Mr. Hernandez?"

"I have my ways. That should be of no concern to you right now. I have much more pressing matters to discuss."

"What do you want?"

"I want to meet with you."

"For what purpose?" Her heartbeat sped up. She had no idea where he was going with this.

Zach was shaking his head no, but she wanted to hear what Mick had to say.

"I don't want to discuss the particulars over the phone."

"Surely you can't expect after all that has happened that I would agree to this?"

"Ms. Hughes, I have no intention of hurting you right now. If I wanted you dead, you'd already be dead. Make no mistake about that. But to alleviate your concerns, we can meet in a public place. You can bring your security entourage with you, but when we talk, it just has to be you and me. I can guarantee it will be more than worth your time."

"Let me think about it." She wanted to buy herself some time.

"There's only one real response here. You and I both know it."

Zach made a hand motion indicating that she had to wrap up the call. He was probably worried about her phone being traced.

"I need some time." She hung up the phone and realized her heart was still pounding.

"Wow. What was that all about?" she asked Zach.

"I don't know, but I can tell you I don't like it." Zach stood and pulled out his phone. "I need to update Brodie about this latest development."

"Aren't you the slightest bit curious about what Mick wants? Why would he contact me and want to meet? What could he possibly want to share with me?"

He frowned. "What he wants is to get you out of the picture before you cause any more trouble for his family. I'm sure he realizes that Ana could be the next person on your list."

"How do you know that? What if he wants to strike some sort of deal?"

Zach laughed loudly. "You can't possibly believe that. You are grasping at straws here, Jess. This is a criminal mastermind we're talking about. There's no way he would do that, especially since he has the upper hand right now. His son was just acquitted. No, he's on top of the world, and not a man in a position to give up any ground. This has to be something else, but I don't know what."

Jessica let Zach phone in the update to Brodie. But there was one thing she was certain of. She didn't care what the FBI thought—she was going to take this meeting with Mick Hernandez.

EIGHT

"I'm going to that meeting." That was a statement of fact. As she looked first at Zach and then Brodie, she hoped that they realized she was serious. She'd talked to Ian last night, and he was in total agreement with her. The prosecutor's office wasn't in any position to turn down meetings with someone like Mick. Even if there was only a remote chance that something would come of it, she had to take it. Ian had told her that he would call Brodie if need be, but she wanted to be able to fight this battle for herself.

There was no doubt in her mind what she was going to do. The only question was whether the FBI was going to provide her security or not. But if she had to go it alone, she would.

"What do you expect to gain from a face-to-face?" Brodie asked.

"You're looking at this all wrong. If Mick Hernandez wants to meet with me, it's not to harm me. There's something else going on here. And it's my duty to figure out what it is. What if this will provide a break in the case?"

"I don't see any scenario in which meeting with Mick will help the case against Ana," Zach argued. "The last thing in the world he would do is turn against his own daughter. That's just a cold, hard fact."

"Even if it's not related to Ana specifically, what if he has some sort of information he wants to share? It's not every day that a crime boss wants to meet with a prosecutor. I'm telling you something is going on here. I have to find out what it is. And Ian feels the exact same way. One part of our job is to take meetings and interviews like this. Even if they are with notorious criminals—in fact, even more so if they are. The prosecutor's office doesn't turn away people who say they want to talk and have information."

"She has a point, you know," Brodie said. "This isn't a social call."

Zach blew out a big breath. "If this is an option that's really on the table, then we'd want to control all the variables, including location and timing of the meet."

"We may not be able to put all of those demands on him," she said.

Zach shook his head. "If he wants to meet you that badly, then he'll make certain concessions."

Her phone rang, and she knew it was Mick wanting her answer. She was almost surprised that he'd given her overnight to think about it. "That's got to be him." She answered and put it on Speaker.

"Ms. Hughes," Mick said.

"Yes. I'm here."

"I assume you've thought about my proposal and given it your full attention?"

"Yes, I have. And if I'm going to seriously entertain it, then I get to pick the time and place."

"I have no issue with that," Mick replied.

She raised an eyebrow toward Zach and Brodie. Something strange was definitely going on.

"Two o'clock today at the Bay Café on Third Street," she said.

"One condition."

Here it comes. "Yes?"

"You can't wear a wire. That's nonnegotiable. Our conversation is solely between you and me. Bring whatever security you want."

"Fine." She answered before the guys could weigh in. "I'll see you then." The line went dead.

She set down the phone and looked at the two men in front of her. Their puzzled expressions let her know that everyone was trying to figure out what Mick's play was here.

"Why in the world did you commit to not wearing a wire?" Brodie asked.

"Because I want him to be forthcoming with me. I have a feeling that this is going to be something big. I don't know what, but I'm comfortable without a wire. You guys and other agents will be right there. Just not at the table with me and Mick."

"You didn't give us much time to prepare," Zach said.

"We'll be fine. The sooner we have this meeting, the better."

"I'm signing off on this but only because you want to do it, Jessica," Zach said. "But you can back out at any point if you feel uncomfortable."

Yeah right, she thought. "That's not going to happen. Don't worry about me having cold feet. I need to know what he's going to say."

"Fair enough. But whatever Mick tells you, remember who he is. His word isn't any good. This man is a liar. Not to mention a cold-blooded murderer."

She nodded. "I won't let down my guard. And you guys will be right there watching my back."

"I'm going to go and start figuring out the logistics for this meeting," Brodie said. "I'll be in touch over the next couple of hours."

Once they were alone, Zach walked over to her and gently rested his hand on her shoulder. It was strange because she was getting used to his touch. She couldn't say that about anyone else, but it actually brought her comfort. And she found herself longing for something more. "What's wrong?" she asked.

"I'm worried about how this is going to go. I'm sorry if you think I'm being overprotective, but it's my job and duty to worry about your well-being."

"I appreciate that, but it's also very strange that Mick Hernandez is insisting on this meeting. If you were in my shoes, you would definitely attend."

He nodded and took a step closer to her. "Jess, I don't want you to take this the wrong way…"

Where was he going with this? "Just say what you're thinking. I'd like to think that we can be open with each other at this point."

"It's just that I care, that's all."

"Of course you care. You're a hardworking, dedicated FBI agent. I wouldn't expect anything else from you. If you would've just sent me off to go meet with Mick alone, then that would be crazy. You're doing your job."

"That's true, but that's not what I meant."

Now she was really confused. "Okay, you've lost me, then. What are you saying?"

He took a deep breath and looked directly into her eyes. "I care about you."

Instinctively, she took a step back from him. It hit her now exactly what he was talking about. Had he sensed her growing feelings for him? She didn't know if she was ready to open up about that given that she wasn't sure if she would ever be able to really act on them. "I don't know what to say."

"You don't have to say anything." He stepped toward her.

And this time she didn't back down. Because she wasn't afraid of this man. Caught off guard, yes, but afraid? Definitely not. In fact, she'd never felt less afraid of someone. But her inexperience was showing. She hadn't noticed the signs that he was interested in her.

"I didn't walk into this looking to form any emotional connection to you, Jess. In fact, that was about the last thing on my mind when we started working together. But somewhere along the way…"

"So you're saying you've developed feelings for me?" She wanted to make certain that she wasn't misunderstanding what he was trying to say because that would be highly embarrassing if she was wrong.

"Yes. But it won't impact my ability to do the job. I would never put your life at risk."

"I never said that it would," she said softly. "But I don't want you to get the wrong idea from me. I've always been on my own. I get that it's very odd for a twenty-five-year-old woman to never have been in a relationship, but there's never been anyone who I felt like I could even begin to trust. As you know, my scars run deep."

His eyes softened. "You can't want to live your entire life that way."

"It's not a question of want, Zach. It's more that it's the only way I know how." She heard her voice crack slightly as the pain of her past threatened to impact her present yet again. She desperately wanted to be able to live in the moment with Zach. But shaking off her fear was difficult. Although he made her want to try to break through her troubled past.

He took one more step toward her. Much closer than she would normally want anyone to be. But there wasn't one hint of danger from this man. And that in and of itself scared her, because what if he was right? Would there be a chance of her having a normal relationship like most people?

"Now it's my turn to ask you what you're thinking?" His voice was low and he didn't break eye contact with her.

As she stared up into his big brown eyes, she wanted to open up to him. Wanted to be close to him. Wanted to feel his tender touch. "Zach…" When he pressed his lips to hers, she heard herself let out a small gasp.

When his lips left hers, she didn't say a word. But she knew one thing. She was in trouble now.

* * *

Zach had kissed Jessica before he'd really thought it through. As he was standing there looking at her, so vulnerable and strong at the same time, he reacted without weighing the pros and cons. It was unlike him to be so spontaneous, but it just felt right. He wanted to ask God if He had brought Jessica into his life for a purpose. Not just to make him a better agent and man, but to provide him with companionship. A woman who shared his beliefs and his passions in life.

Right now he was in overanalyzing mode. What did she really think about him? And even more than that, was it even appropriate for him to have kissed her while they were focusing on this big meeting with Mick?

He didn't regret it. The kiss confirmed to him what he already felt in his gut. That Jessica was special. He realized that she had a lot of issues in her past that made it difficult for her to open up, or even receive affection of any kind, but he believed he could overcome that. Maybe he was foolish for thinking so, but he couldn't help it.

Now as he sat with her in the SUV waiting to go inside the Bay Café, he wondered if he should act as though nothing happened or try to broach the subject. Other plainclothes FBI agents were scoping out the café and would provide security. It wasn't time yet for Jessica to go inside.

"So do you want to talk about what happened back there?"

"What do you mean?"

Ah, so that's how she was going to play it. Pure denial. "C'mon, Jess. The kiss."

"Yeah," she stuttered. "I wasn't really expecting that."

"Are we okay?" He hoped the answer would be a solid yes.

"Of course. Don't you think our bigger problem right now is this meeting with Mick? Not a silly little kiss."

"Ouch," he said. "Way to slam the blade right into a guy's heart."

Her shoulders relaxed, and she looked at him. "I'm sorry. I didn't mean it like that. I'm in unfamiliar territory right now. It's not you."

"But it's not you, either, Jess."

"I appreciate you saying that, but I think this was the first time you've been a bit dishonest with me."

"What in the world do you mean?"

"You and I both know that I have some serious issues. A person doesn't experience the things I did and come out on the other side perfectly fine. Yeah, I manage, and I know a lot of that is because I have my faith to get me through. But in the grand scheme of things, you'd be much better off if you just walked away and found a woman who didn't flinch when you touched her. Who didn't have nightmares all the time. Who didn't constantly live on edge and ready to fight another battle. I don't want to hold you back from true happiness."

It killed him to hear her say those things. To him, she was perfect just the way she was. "Don't you see, Jess? All of those things make you who you are today. A strong, amazing woman. I wouldn't change a single thing about you. And as far as your past, we all have issues that shape who we are. But they don't have to hold us back unless we let them. And I don't think you're a victim but a fighter. Just look at all you've accomplished and overcome. The past doesn't have to keep a grip on you today."

"That's easier said than done, Zach. I can't just shake it off."

"And I wouldn't ever ask you to. I don't know how to exactly say this, but I think you're your own harshest critic."

She let out a breath. "I don't know where any of that leaves us."

"I don't want to get you off your game here. We can talk about it later. Just know that it wasn't just a little kiss to me. It meant a lot more than that."

"Really?" Her bright green eyes studied him carefully.

He reached out and touched her hand. "Really." He paused. "Now let's get you inside and get this show on the road."

Jessica was still reeling from the kiss. She was out of her comfort zone, and she felt torn because she did have feelings for Zach. But she also didn't know if her heart could ever truly be open to a man—even if he was amazing like Zach.

She had to compartmentalize. Thankfully, it was a skill she had mastered years ago.

Right now she had a meeting with one of the most notorious crime bosses in the state. She'd played in her mind a million times all the things she'd like to ask him, but she wasn't naive. She knew that this wasn't a Q&A session or an interrogation. No, this was something else. Mick wanted an audience with the prosecutor—her specifically—but she wasn't sure what that could mean. She was about to find out.

Jessica looked down at her watch and saw that it was one minute before two o'clock. She sat at a corner table near an exit that was protected by a plainclothes FBI agent. Zach was sitting at a high-top table nearby, keeping his eyes on her. Close but not too close.

Taking a few deep breaths, Jessica readied herself for whatever may come. She watched the door as Mick Hernandez walked in. He was alone, but she figured his men couldn't be far.

He appeared just as he had in the pictures she'd seen. A tall man in his sixties, with a full head of gray hair, dressed in a white button-down, navy blazer and khakis. He looked more like a businessman going out for afternoon coffee—not a calculating criminal.

When he made eye contact with her, he broke into a sinister smile—one that made her question whether this was a good decision after all. But she wasn't going to let this man intimidate or play mind games with her. She was prepared to deal with whatever he threw at her. It also helped that Zach was only a few feet away—not to mention all the other agents.

"Ms. Hughes, so nice to meet you in person." He stretched out his hand.

She took it because it seemed awkward not to. He gave her a hearty shake and took a seat.

"I trust that you aren't wearing a wire?"

"You're just going to take my word for it?" she asked him.

"You're an honest woman, Ms. Hughes. We had an agreement. So if you look me in the eyes and tell me that you're not, then yes, I will believe you."

"I'm not wearing a wire."

"I appreciate that."

Time to cut the pleasantries and get down to business. "Mr. Hernandez, I must say I'm a bit puzzled over why you wanted to meet with me."

"I can imagine that you are." Mick leaned forward in his seat. "I promise this won't be a waste of your time, though. I know how busy you are in the prosecutor's office. Especially after the acquittal. I can imagine that you're trying to find your next target."

She shook her head. "I don't have targets, Mr. Hernandez. I go where the evidence and facts take me. Wherever that may be, even if there are obstacles in my way."

He cocked his head to the side. "Well, you seem quite intent on prosecuting my children."

"I don't really think it's appropriate to go down this road and have this discussion, and I find it hard to believe that's why you called me here today."

He crossed his arms. "Actually, that's exactly why I called you here."

"I'm sorry—I don't follow." She had no idea what he was talking about.

"Since you're so intent on prosecuting my children, then I figured you'd want to hear what I have to say."

"You're speaking in riddles, Mr. Hernandez. Why don't you just tell me whatever it is, and we'll go from there." She was quickly becoming exasperated with his tactics.

"If you want someone to investigate, then you should be looking at Luke."

"As in your son?" Okay, now he'd thrown her for a loop.

His lips turned up into a smile. "See, I knew you would be interested."

"I didn't say I was interested. I'm surprised. Luke is a law-abiding member of the community. A Miami PD detective. So you'll have to excuse my skepticism here. Especially coming from you."

"I expected you to have that exact reaction. Which is why I wanted to meet with you face-to-face and have this discussion. I have evidence implicating Luke in a nasty corruption scheme. You do realize that good cops turn bad all the time."

She had a hard time believing any of this. Mick had an agenda here. "And why in the world would you come to me to try to rat out your own son?"

"You need to understand the context to fully appreciate the situation."

"All right. I'm listening."

"My family is the most important thing to me in my life. So this isn't something I take lightly at all."

"But you still want me to—what? Investigate your son?"

"That's what I am explaining to you. For me to be at this point, you have to realize how serious it has become. Luke sold out the family a long time ago. I have given him plenty of opportunities to ask for forgiveness, to change his ways. But after a long time, it became apparent to me that he was actively working against the rest of us. The only thing stopping me from acting against him sooner is because his mother has a soft spot for him. But I can't turn away from this opportunity because things have escalated a bit and gotten out of control. Luke has to be stopped."

"Let me get this straight. You want me to prosecute your son?" She was having a hard time even having this discussion with him.

"That's right. I'll provide the evidence, and then you can do your prosecutorial thing."

There was always going to be a catch. She knew that. "And I take it you want something in exchange?"

He laughed. "I want you to leave the rest of my family, including my daughter, alone."

"You know I can't do that."

His expression turned serious very quickly. "You can and you will."

"Are you threatening me, Mr. Hernandez?"

"That was merely a statement of fact. You're barking up the wrong tree, Ms. Hughes. What I'm bringing to you is so much bigger than anything else you would ever be able to do against my family."

"Okay." She was going to play along for the time being and see what she could find out. "Let's just say okay for the sake of argument. What precisely are you claiming that Luke is involved in?"

"He's part of a ring of dirty cops playing both sides

of the drug scene. They're skimming products, taking the extra cash from the busts and all sorts of other things."

As she looked into Mick's eyes, she wondered if there could be any truth to these allegations. "How do I know that you're telling the truth?"

"I wouldn't waste my time otherwise. If I was fabricating this story, you'd find out eventually and this would've been a silly exercise. That wouldn't help me or you."

"Okay, then. And where is this so-called evidence?"

"I have it. But you see—there's something else."

"Another catch? You sure are attaching a lot of strings here."

"I don't want any of this traced back to me. My wife wouldn't forgive me. As far as everyone else is concerned, this meeting is about me telling you to back off."

"Then how are you getting your revenge? Isn't that what this is all about?"

"This is much bigger than revenge."

A chill shot down her back at his calculating grin. There was no doubt in her mind that this man would make good on his threats. He was selling out his own son to a prosecutor. It made her sick. But what concerned her even more was whether there was any truth to his allegations. Or was this just a way for Mick to try to get her off her investigation into Ana?

"If I were interested in seeing this evidence? How would that happen?"

He reached into his jacket pocket and pulled out a

thumb drive. He slid it across the table to her. Before she could grab it, he put his hand on hers. She flinched.

"Aren't you a jumpy one?" he asked. "Although I guess after all that has happened, it's to be expected."

He assumed that she jumped because of the current threats against her. He had no idea it went much deeper than that. And she was glad for it.

Jessica pulled away from him quickly and put the thumb drive into her purse. "I'll take a look in the same way I'd evaluate evidence against any other person. There will be absolutely no special consideration because of this conversation. As far as I'm concerned, it's just like any other case."

"I'm confident that when you see what's on there, there will be an indictment forthcoming against multiple members of the Miami PD—including Luke."

"I'll be the judge of that." His bravado bothered her. What if he actually had something here? The idea that Luke Hernandez was a dirty cop was not something she wanted to entertain, but now it appeared that she wouldn't have a choice. Would Mick really orchestrate such an elaborate ruse if there was nothing to it? She didn't know. Staring into his eyes right now, he looked deadly serious.

"I'm sure that there will be charges brought because I can tell that you're a rule follower. You're young and naive enough to think that it's always about doing the so-called right thing. You have integrity and a blind sense of justice. For my current purposes, you're the perfect prosecutor to take down my son."

She didn't have a comeback because it was pointless

to try to argue that she wouldn't follow the law—they both knew that she would.

"I think we're done here." Jessica let out a deep breath when Mick stood up from his chair. Then he turned around and looked over his shoulder. "And don't forget what I said about Ana. She's off-limits. For good."

Her meeting with one of the biggest crime bosses in Miami was over. And his message was clear. If she went after Ana, he'd be coming after her. But her first problem would be explaining to the FBI everything that had just transpired.

Zach walked over to the table. "Let's get out of here. We can talk en route back to the safe house."

Jessica used the time it took to get escorted out to the vehicle to regain her composure and think about how she'd present the facts to Zach. She knew he was going to immediately pounce on this.

Once in the SUV, Zach glanced over at her. "Okay, give it to me. What happened? I want to hear everything. It looked like an intense conversation judging from both of your body language."

"You're right—it was. But I wasn't afraid."

"What did you talk about?"

"Before I tell you, I need you to promise me that you won't jump to any hasty conclusions." She didn't want him to immediately convict Luke before they even knew all the facts or had viewed the evidence.

"Is that something I normally do?"

"I think you will on this, Zach. That's why I wanted to preface what I'm going to say with that. Please just hear me out."

"Of course."

"All right. Mick wanted to talk to me because he had evidence he wanted to give me."

"Evidence about what?"

She took another breath. There was no point in trying to back into this. Better to just say it. "He wants me to make a case against Luke."

"What?" Zach asked loudly. "Are you serious?"

"Yes. That's why I didn't want you to jump to conclusions. You've had it out for Luke since the beginning. But we need to examine all the facts before any actions are taken."

"Wow," Zach said. "What evidence does he have? What's the allegation? I have so many questions."

"Let's take it one step at a time."

"Good idea. Walk me through the entire meeting."

"I told him I was surprised that he asked to meet with me. Then he said that since I was so focused on targeting his children, he had something to offer me."

"And he gave up his own kid, just like that?"

"Well, not without strings attached. He basically said that I should prosecute Luke, not Ana. And he threatened me if I continued with anything against her."

"You're thinking this is a ruse to try to protect his little girl."

"It was my first thought, but unfortunately there is more."

"Go on."

"He gave me a jump drive that he claims has evidence on it specifically implicating Luke and other Miami PD officers in some sort of illegal drug ring."

Zach whistled. "This is huge, Jessica. I'm sure that given the gravity of these allegations, Brodie will brief Special Agent in Charge Cox. Since this is an allegation against Miami PD, we need to keep them walled off from this."

"We're getting ahead of ourselves. This could all be nothing. A trick to try to divert our attention away from the real criminal here."

"Or all of his children are dirty. But just thinking out loud here. Why would Mick turn against Luke if his son was truly on the dark side?"

"Good question. When I asked him about it, he said it was because Luke had sold out the family. I think he was alluding to the fact that Luke has not been loyal to them. There's a backstory there that he didn't get into."

"I know you don't want me to jump to conclusions, but we can't just ignore these allegations because they came from Mick and might be self-serving. It could be that they have merit and Mick was also using that to his strategic advantage."

They pulled up to the safe house. Jessica knew their conversation was far from over. "I agree that we have to investigate. I need to look at what is on this jump drive ASAP."

"I want to get one of the FBI tech guys to make sure there isn't malware or anything else on there first. The last thing we would need is for the Hernandez family to infiltrate our computer network. We should follow our normal protocol here."

"The analysis of the jump drive has to happen right away."

"Believe me. I have the same sense of urgency that you do. If there's a police corruption scheme, it's going to be a mess. I'll call our tech people now, plus Brodie."

She didn't know where this path was going to lead, but she'd have to follow it.

As she settled down on the living room couch, Zach started making phone calls. She took the few minutes and started making a list of everything that Mick had told her while it was fresh in her mind. Having this meeting documented was going to be important. What she really wanted was to get access to that jump drive and review the evidence. But she completely understood that they needed to take precautions.

She was relieved when members from the FBI tech team arrived at the safe house and started their analysis. Now all she could do was wait.

When Zach rushed into the room a bit later, she knew something was up.

"We've got a problem," he said.

"What's wrong?" she asked.

"Luke Hernandez is missing."

NINE

"What do you mean he's missing?" Jessica asked while her mind raced with possibilities.

"He didn't report in for duty today, and there's no sign of him at his house," Zach said.

"Do you think Mick decided to take matters into his own hands? That wouldn't make much sense." The puzzle pieces weren't clicking for her.

"No. I don't think that at all. I think it's more likely that Luke is guilty, and he realized he was about to be exposed, so he hit the road."

"Or he could be in danger. Maybe he's on the run because he's worried about what his father will do."

Zach shook his head. "I understand that you wanted to give Luke a fair shake, but in the face of the conversation you had with Mick and when the evidence he's given you pans out, we have to start working under the assumption that Luke is not clean."

As much as she hated to admit it, Zach was right. "I hear you. What exactly are you suggesting?"

"The FBI techs are working on the drive now. As

soon as they're done, we can start looking at what's on there and see where that takes us."

"Regardless of what happens with Luke, I don't plan to stop our investigation into Ana."

"I don't see any reason why we shouldn't go after both of them. Assuming, of course, that our bosses agree."

"I'm pretty sure that Ian will want to follow the evidence—wherever that takes us is where he'll want to go. But if there is anything going on with Luke that exposes a big and thorny issue with the Miami PD, then I realize that could get super dicey. Especially the citywide politics that could be at play. So I know Ian will want to be involved. I wanted to be able to find out what was on that drive before I called to brief him."

He looked down at his watch. "They should be done with their review any minute now. Let me go check."

Jessica took a seat on the couch and tried to wrap her head around everything. Was it really possible that Luke Hernandez was a dirty cop after all? It bothered her that her instincts about him could've been so far off. But she still wanted to review everything before declaring him guilty. She knew Zach was right, though. At some point things just didn't add up and you had to face the facts in front of you, even if they were unpleasant.

After a few minutes, Zach returned with a laptop in his hand.

"They copied the files to this computer for us to review."

"Great. Let's get to it."

He motioned toward the hallway. "We can use the dining room table.

"I'm assuming you'll want to drive this operation," he said as he took the seat beside her at the table.

"Thanks." Jessica opened the laptop and saw the file folder on the desktop. "Here we go." She took a deep breath as she double-clicked on the file. The folder contained a slew of picture files, spreadsheets and some other documents. She went to the pictures and clicked on the first one.

An image filled the screen. "That's Luke Hernandez, but who is that man with him?" The two men stood together in what appeared to be the back of a tall building. The picture had captured them exchanging a legal-size manila envelope.

"I know him," Zach said.

"You do?"

"Yes. That is Ivan Markov." Zach frowned deeply.

"And who in the world is Ivan Markov?" she asked.

"One of the biggest players in the Russian organized crime syndicates in the country."

"What?"

"Yeah. This just went from huge to epic, Jessica."

"But how do we know that the picture is legitimate?"

"Our experts will be able to determine that."

Thoughts raced through her head. "How do you know this Markov guy?"

"We did a case study on him at Quantico. He's the real deal, Jess. If Luke is involved with Markov, then this is even more serious than I thought."

She opened up the next picture, and there was Luke

again with Markov. This time they were sitting together on a park bench. "How would Luke have even gotten connected with Markov in the first place?"

"Before Luke went to homicide, he did a stint in the drug unit. I imagine that's how he and Markov met. Markov is a big player in the drug business on a national level. But he also has a huge foothold in Miami. Mick would love to get a chunk of that business." Zach looked her in the eyes. "And this makes even more sense now as to why Mick would bring this information to you."

"What do you mean?"

"Because Ivan Markov is Mick's competition in the drug trafficking business. He gets to kill two birds with one stone. Take down his son, who has clearly sold out and is not only working against the Hernandez family but working for and with the Russians. It couldn't be a bigger slap in the face. But it looks like Mick has outsmarted them all and found a way to get at them at the same time—which would ultimately further the Hernandez agenda, especially as it relates to moving up in the drug trade. It will pave the way for Ana to do the work."

"Wow. This is so much bigger than anything I expected. I've got to talk to Ian about this."

"We need to get everyone in one room to discuss our options."

"You do realize that this doesn't make Ana any less guilty."

"I'm with you. I say we take the whole crooked family down."

She flipped through the rest of the pictures, and they

all told the same story—that Luke and Markov were tight. She didn't find any pictures of other police officers. This set of photos was limited to just the two men. There were a variety of shots in different places, but the takeaway was that this wasn't a one-off meeting between the two men. No, they had met multiple times on a variety of different turfs.

An idea occurred to her that she wanted to bounce off Zach. "Is there any possibility that Luke is working on an undercover operation for the Miami police? Or working in conjunction with the DEA or another agency?"

"You know, anything is possible, but that's easy enough to verify quickly."

"I already know that you think he's dirty, but I don't want to jump to conclusions without doing all of our due diligence."

"Don't worry about that. We'll get to the bottom of this."

Later that night, the safe house was a hive of activity. Zach knew things were really getting serious when he was told that Ford Cox was going to be coming over for the meeting. If the head of the FBI Miami field office was involved, then that let him know how important this was. Ford didn't insert himself into investigations unless they were major and high profile.

Zach just hoped that they weren't going to take him off these cases because he was a rookie. He had to prove that he could juggle both investigations if that's what the higher-ups ended up wanting to do.

Jessica wore a deep frown and hadn't said a whole lot since they'd finished reviewing all the evidence. The documents and spreadsheets appeared to show a money trail that led back to some offshore bank accounts. One thing was for sure; it wasn't looking good for Luke Hernandez right now. And while it was true that Zach had always been suspicious of the man, he certainly didn't gain any joy out of discovering how dirty Luke appeared to be.

When Ford Cox walked in, Zach rose and shook his hand. He'd only met Ford in person once before, right when he'd started. The tall, gray-haired special agent in charge was known to be tough, and he ran the Miami office like a very tight ship. While some other SACs might look the other way if there were minor indiscretions among agents, that wasn't how Ford operated.

"Hope I didn't hold things up too much," Ford said. Zach introduced him to Jessica, and they all took their seats.

"Okay, who is going to fill me in?" Ford asked.

Zach looked toward the woman he was quickly falling for. "Jessica, why don't you brief us on what happened in the meeting today?"

"Sure," she said. "Mick Hernandez requested a meeting with me. We set it up, and once he arrived, Mick basically told me to stop investigating his daughter, Ana. He insinuated that if I didn't, he would come after me. But then he told me that he could give me something much more valuable to us. He handed me a jump drive that he said had incriminating evidence against his son—Miami police detective Luke Hernandez. As you can imagine, I was skeptical that this was some sort of ploy to try to throw the investigation off Ana, but I'm sure you've heard that we found some disturbing information in what Mick provided me. This includes pictures and evidence showing a strong tie between Luke and Russian crime boss Ivan Markov."

Ford nodded. "And I'm glad we're all in one room so we can share our knowledge. What I'm about to tell you doesn't leave this room, because there are a lot of moving parts and we can't compromise our active operations— especially ones that we've been working so hard on for years. What everyone here needs to know is that we've been trying to take Ivan Markov down now for the past two years. Up to this point, the guy has been completely untouchable. So this latest development is of great interest to me and my team members working the Markov cases. These guys and gals literally eat, sleep and breathe Markov. And I must say that I spend a big chunk of my time managing our efforts. So what happened here is a big breakthrough that could have some pretty huge ramifications."

Ian leaned forward in his chair. "From our perspective at the prosecutor's office, we just want to be making the strongest cases we can. Obviously, if the evidence pans out against Luke, then we'll take that ball and run with it. But we also don't want to lose sight of Ana Hernandez. I feel like Jessica and Zach are making progress on that investigation, and now isn't the time to back off just because Mick came to us with documents that may incriminate his son."

"And I wouldn't presume to tell you how to do your

job," Ford put in. "But I can tell you from an FBI perspective, Markov is at the top of our list—far above Ana. Yeah, Ana may be trying to expand her drug business, but Markov *is* the drug business in South Florida. And it doesn't stop at drugs, either—he has his hands in everything. So from my end, we will work every angle we can to get hard evidence implicating Markov in the drug business and any other illegal enterprise."

"If I may," Zach ventured. "I don't think these two things have to be mutually exclusive."

"Right," Ford said. "I already have a Markov team in place. They can take point in the investigation regarding Luke. But given the circumstances, we'll need some assistance from you, Zach. And you, too, Jessica."

Zach was thankful that he wasn't being cut out or reassigned. He wanted to be in on the action.

"And what about the Miami PD?" Jessica asked. "How are you going to handle their role in this?"

"Good question," Brodie noted. "I think they are on the sidelines. We will obviously need their help on factual issues and running down things, but we can't have them investigate Luke because we don't know who else is implicated in this illegal scheme."

"Mick said that this involved multiple people at Miami PD," Jessica said. "But the evidence turned over was strictly limited to his son and Markov. It's possible that Mick was just bluffing about the full-on conspiracy to ensure that I would take him seriously."

Ian cleared his throat. "I hate to bring this up, but has anyone considered that Mick Hernandez might be sending us all on a wild-goose chase here?"

"Our FBI experts are analyzing the photos now," Zach told him. "We contacted DEA, and Luke isn't working undercover with them. If the photos check out, then that's pretty compelling proof that Luke is working with Markov. What we don't know from the pictures is what exactly the two of them are up to."

"It's just a bit convenient that Mick brought this to me now, though," Jessica said.

"No doubt he's using us to do his dirty work in a vendetta against his son," Ford said. "But at the end of the day, it benefits us to take these accusations seriously. If things go our way, then maybe we get to take down two criminal families."

"Sounds like we should all get to work, then," Brodie said. "We'll defer to you, Ford, on how you want to run the Markov and Luke case, and we'll provide whatever assistance is needed."

"Let me touch base with my team and fill them in on everything that has happened. Then I'll let everyone know what we need from you," Ford said. "And in the meantime, Zach, you keep working on Ana, and we'll see what we can put together."

After a few minutes of small talk, the group broke up with everyone calling it a night and leaving Zach alone with Jessica once again.

"How do you think that went?" he asked.

"Ford really has his sights set on Markov. Hopefully that won't cloud his judgment as far as Luke's involvement goes."

"Ford didn't get to be in his position today by letting

his emotions sway him. He's thought to be one of the best SACs in the nation."

"I get that Ford has his special team focusing on Markov, but we have to stay relevant. I don't want to get totally iced out of the Luke investigation. I need to know what kind of legal case I could make against him if it comes to that."

"Believe me, everyone knows that the prosecutor's office has to have a key role no matter how things shake out."

"Well, at least we have the green light to continue our work with Ana. You know that Mick won't be happy about that."

"He won't. Which means we need to be particularly cautious. And it would also be good if he thinks that you're aggressively following up on the Luke leads. Maybe that could give us a little breathing room as far as Mick's concerned."

"That's a good point," Jessica acknowledged. "And just between you and me, I'd like to do some of my own independent investigation into Luke and Markov."

Zach wasn't sure if that was a good idea. "Don't you think we need to stick to protocol?"

She raised an eyebrow. "I'm not saying that we should mess with Ford's work—I'm just thinking that I'd like to follow up on a few points myself."

He reached out and squeezed her hand. "Nothing else can be done tonight." What he really wanted to do was bring her into his arms and kiss her again. But he knew better. He didn't want to move too quickly and scare her away.

"You're right. I'm worn-out. Let's get some rest and we can get a full day's work in tomorrow."

Jessica had given it a lot of thought, and she wanted to make sure that she was getting to the bottom of this maze of organized crime. Yeah, Ford gave his FBI orders, but she didn't work for the bureau. She intended to work both cases and find the truth. There was still a nagging feeling deep within her that something was off. That Luke was being set up. But she was clearly in the minority in that belief. And she couldn't make her opinion known too loudly or else they might cut her out altogether. No, she just needed some time to look into everything herself.

Dressed and ready to go, she walked into the kitchen to find that Zach was also up and drinking coffee.

"Good morning," he said.

"I've been thinking," she countered.

"Uh-oh." He smiled. "What's on your mind?"

"I want to go down to the harbor today and check it out. Remember what Will said. There's still a chance that something is going on this weekend with Ana's drug operation. And I don't want to lose that opportunity. Something could be happening right now."

"I don't think you'll see anything in broad daylight at the marina or at the dock. Unless we have actionable evidence to open up those shipping containers and carts, we might as well be looking at crates full of legal materials. Without a warrant, it would be a futile exercise."

She poured coffee for herself and looked into Zach's

eyes. "What's your suggestion, then? We've been given the green light to keep up our work."

"If you're totally set on looking to see what is happening at the harbor, then we should at least wait until nightfall and then do some recon. The tip from Will was vague. We don't know the location of this supposed event that's going to go down. It could be at one their front businesses and not at the harbor."

"If you think the harbor trip isn't worthwhile, then I'd like to scope out her establishments. We don't have to wait until tonight to do that, do we?"

"No. We can do that now if you'd like. But we can only accomplish so much."

"I haven't even seen these two places. I'd like to at least survey the scene and check for anything suspicious. It can't hurt to take a look."

"All right. You ready?" he asked.

"Yes. I'm eager to get to work," she answered.

By the time they had reached the area of town where Ana's dry cleaning business was, Jessica had become anxious. Yes, it was her idea to do this, but she started to get a little worried that Mick might have his men on the lookout for her.

"The dry cleaner's is a few blocks away. I'll park in this public lot and we can walk around."

She took in her surroundings. "I don't know what I expected, but this isn't really it," she said.

"Yeah, a bit more upscale than what you would assume for a criminal enterprise. But that's the way for the Hernandez family," Zach said. "We'll look around here, and then we can take it from there. Mainly I just want to get the lay of the land."

"I got it."

"And stay close to me. Even though Mick seems to have called a mini-truce so that you can take down Luke doesn't mean Ana or Simon feel the same way."

"I know there's going to be risks involved here. I've come to terms with that, and I'm not afraid. Anxious maybe but not scared."

"Because God has your back."

"Yes. He's got both of our backs. That doesn't mean I'm going to be careless, but I'm also not going to live in fear." She stuck close by his side as they walked in silence for three blocks. Jessica remained vigilant and aware of her surroundings, and she could tell that Zach was, as well. They were both focused on the job they needed to get done. She wasn't naive enough to think that she was totally in the clear from threats.

"It's going to be up ahead on the right," he said.

She looked up toward where the dry cleaner's was, and then she suddenly stopped short and took his hand in hers, squeezing hard. "Wait."

"What's wrong?" he asked. He immediately stopped walking.

"That's Ana Hernandez right there, walking out of the store and headed this way. Straight toward us. We can't let her see that we're down here."

"Come on," he said. He grabbed tightly on to her arm. They crossed the street and started walking away from Ana.

"That was close," she said. Her heartbeat thumped wildly.

"Yeah, we'll do a loop and then come back."

She tried to focus on steadying her breathing. "Do you think she saw us?"

He shook his head. "I don't think so."

They were walking at a rapid pace, and she didn't want to turn around and look to see where Ana was. "I guess that means she's actually an active business owner and doesn't just operate from afar."

"There isn't any doubt that she's operating a legitimate business. The issue is what else is she running through there and how do we get proof of it."

Suddenly an idea struck her. "What if we could befriend someone who works in the dry cleaner's?"

"It's a good idea, but that would mean one of Ana's workers turning on her. I'd say there's zero chance of that happening."

"We'd have to offer them something that would make it worth it."

"I don't know, Jess. Given the reputation of the family, I can't imagine it would be that feasible to turn someone unless they had something major and we could give them a new life. I doubt either of those things would be possible for one of her employees."

"Well, there's already one CI. Why not develop another source? Especially since I'm in the dark on the details of the one that's in play."

"As I explained before, it normally takes years of working for the family before you'd get access to any actionable evidence that would be worth something to us to be a legal case."

"Okay, but what about if it's not someone who is a CI or turns on Ana? What if we just try to look for an inside source that we can work for information? Maybe not hard evidence per se that we'd use to make our case, but general intel on the operations that could lead us to a bust. It's possible that one of Ana's employees might know something without even realizing it. If we ask the right questions, we might just find something that could help us out."

"I think that idea is much more workable. But the two of us can't just stroll in there together and start asking questions. And for all we know, Ana has the place under surveillance."

"How about we stand watch until one of the people who works there leaves for lunch or at the end of their shift?"

"I like that thought, but I still think only one of us should talk to them. And only if the opportunity presents itself where it would make sense. There are a lot of variables at play here."

As they made their way back around the extended loop and toward the store, Jessica was feeling as though they had a solid plan. "I'm feeling good about this. Like we actually have something we can start working on in addition to trying to build a case from the paper records that the FBI has accumulated."

"I do, too. Now we'll just need to hone in on the right person and hope for the best."

They walked toward the dry cleaner's and then

paused at the stoplight, waiting for it to change so they could cross the street.

When the white walk sign lit up, Jessica started to cross the street with Zach close by her side.

She was startled by the sound of screeching tires. When she looked up, Jessica saw that a dark SUV was plowing ahead through the red light and headed straight for them.

TEN

Zach saw the oncoming SUV and acted on pure instinct as he grabbed Jessica into his arms, ran a few
steps and then rolled to the safety of the sidewalk.

He let out a breath as he saw the vehicle fly by, missing them by only a few steps.

"Are you all right?" he asked.

She looked at him with wide eyes but didn't speak.
Her breathing was ragged, and he could feel her taking breaths as her shoulders rose and fell. A few people
gathered around the area, but surprisingly they hadn't
drawn that much attention to themselves.

"Jessica," he said. "Are you hurt? Speak to me."

"I..." she stuttered. "I don't know."

He realized that she might be going into shock. They
had hit the ground hard. His top priority had been trying to save Jessica's life. But that had been entirely
too close. Thank the Lord that he'd been able to react.
"Jess, I'm going to help you up off the sidewalk. Can
you try to stand?"

"I think so," she said softly.

He didn't think she had major physical injuries, but was more affected emotionally from what had just happened. He couldn't blame her. But he had to be strong enough for the both of them right now.

Slowly he helped lift her off the sidewalk and onto her feet. "How are you feeling now?"

"Wow," she said. "That was surreal. Like out of a movie."

"Much too close if you ask me. Are you able to walk?"

She took a step and nodded. "Yes. Nothing feels like it's broken. But that was a hard fall. Will probably be a bit sore."

He took her hand in his. "I'm so sorry about that."

"Don't apologize. If you hadn't acted, I'd be much worse off. Probably dead."

He didn't even want to think about that. "All right. This recon session is over for now. I need to get you back to the safe house so we can figure out what in the world is going on."

"Why would Mick send someone after me so soon? He wants me working the case against Luke."

"Maybe it wasn't directly from Mick. It could've come from Simon or Ana. Or Mick could've already been tipped off that you were nosing around down here in Ana's territory and sent someone."

"I still can't believe that if you hadn't acted so quickly…"

"That's why I'm here." He was thankful that he had been able to act. There was always that piece of doubt inside him as to whether he was truly ready after he finished Quantico.

"Thank God you were."

"I'm just glad you're okay."

"I'll feel a lot better once we get back to the safe house." She squeezed his hand tightly. He felt a fierce need to protect her at all costs.

On the drive back, he gave her a few minutes to calm down and get her head around what had happened. "This was too dangerous," he said. "I miscalculated the threat, thinking it would be fine to do the recon near Ana's place. Obviously I was wrong about that."

"You couldn't have known."

"I should have, though. Another rookie mistake." He gripped the wheel, upset that he'd taken an unnecessary risk with Jessica. "They're starting to add up on me."

"Don't be too hard on yourself, Zach. I think we all thought that Mick was going to lay off me and that he's the one ultimately calling the shots. We didn't place enough weight on what Ana and Simon might do if left to their own devices."

"We'll need to let everyone know what happened. I'll have to deal with the fallout of my decision to take you down there in the first place. This might get me removed from the case."

She reached over and touched his arm lightly. "Zach, you literally just saved my life. I think you should give yourself a break. We still don't know exactly what is going on and who tried to take me out. And we were told to continue our investigation. How were we expected to do that unless we got out there and tried to run down leads?"

"After this attack, the uncertainty just fuels my thinking that we have to go back into more of a lock-down mode."

"But once again, how can we investigate out of the safe house?"

"I know you're upset, but we can still do a lot from there. And I'm not saying we can't do other things, but going back into the hornets' nest probably isn't the best thing. The whole block could be covered with Hernandez cameras."

Jessica didn't respond, and he watched as she leaned her head back against the seat and closed her eyes. He didn't know whether she was resting or thinking or praying. So he just let her be.

When they arrived back to the safe house, Jessica said she needed a few minutes alone. And he totally got that. This attempt on her life had been far too close of a call. They'd let down their guards an inch, and this was the result. He wouldn't make that mistake again—that was for sure.

He'd texted Brodie to stop by. When his supervisor got there, Zach recounted the entire series of events to him.

"Why did you think it was a good idea to go down to the dry cleaner's? What did you hope to gain?" Brodie frowned.

Before Zach could respond, Brodie kept on talking.

"I guess sometimes I have to remind myself that you're the new kid. You've handled so much up to this point—even the mishap in the courtroom really was understandable to me. But I need to be more involved to help prevent you from making these kinds of errors. I don't have to tell you how costly this could've been."

"I deserve all of this," Zach said. "I get that. But we also need to think about the nature of the threat, and how it fits within the bigger puzzle."

"Where's Jessica?" Brodie asked.

"She's in her room. This really shook her up. We took quite a tumble out there. It was the only way to save her life."

"I don't know what Ian and Ford will want to do, but my guess is that they'll want Jessica to stay here until we know more of what's going on."

"Yeah. Do you think that Mick would come after her again this soon even if he realized she was down there by Ana's business?"

"I can see him sending out a warning shot, but this sounds more like a direct hit to me. I doubt Mick would've gone through this whole song and dance with Jessica just to turn around and order her to be taken out. If I had to say, I'd think it's more likely someone working for Ana because the woman has to know that she's the next one on Jessica's list. And yeah, Mick runs the show, but nothing stops his kids from making their own decisions. Especially if Ana feels like no one has her back here and that Jessica is on her trail. But if Mick knew that you two were snooping around down there, he wouldn't be happy. We need to tighten this up before it's too late."

"I agree with you," Zach said.

"What are you guys talking about?" Jessica slowly entered the kitchen. It was obvious to him that she was in a bit of pain given her awkward steps. But thankfully the color had come back to her cheeks. She was one tough woman.

"Jessica, I'm so glad that you're okay," Brodie told her.

"Thank you. It's all because of Zach though. If it wasn't for his quick thinking, I wouldn't be standing here talking to you right now."

She looked over at him, and he felt his heart constrict just a bit. "Thank you," he said. There was no doubt in his mind that Jessica was much more to him than just his assignment. He cared for this woman. Keeping her safe meant everything to him. He wouldn't let her down again by allowing her to be in the crosshairs.

"Zach and I were talking about who could've been behind this attack today," Brodie said. "It doesn't really matter because as far as I'm concerned the FBI position will be that you need to lay low, Jessica. There's still a target on your back, and the threats could be coming from multiple fronts."

She looked at Brodie. "I still need to be able to do my job, though. To be able to put together cases, just like I was tasked to do."

"No one is saying you can't work your cases," Brodie said. "But we have to have some stronger ground rules for what kind of work you should be doing outside the safety of this place. Today could've gone a totally different direction as you very well know."

She nodded. "I just hate to feel like I'm on the sidelines if I could do something more."

"You're far from the sidelines, Jessica," Zach said. "But going directly into enemy territory is something else entirely."

"I also think we're about ready to move you to a new safe house. There's been plenty of activity here lately. I'd be more comfortable with another move," Brodie said.

"Have you heard anything else about Luke?" Jessica asked.

"Nothing," Brodie answered. "They're doing their best to track him down, but right now the trail is cold. That's the thing with someone like Luke. He's a cop, so he knows every trick in the book."

"I know you two don't want to hear this, but I still wonder if he's fled because he knows he's in danger—from all fronts."

"Hopefully, we can find him and he can answer all of those questions and more for us," Brodie said. "Before it's too late."

Jessica had accepted changing safe houses again. Although it seemed that just when she'd get comfortable in one place, they'd want to move. But after what had happened yesterday, she couldn't really blame the FBI for being more cautious. If she was being honest with herself, that attempt on her life had totally shaken her up. It wasn't the first time they'd come after her, but if Zach hadn't been on top of his game, she'd be dead.

She had no doubt that the Lord was protecting her.

Yes, Zach had done his part, but God had been watching over both of them yesterday. If they needed to take more precautions for the sake of safety, she wasn't in a position to complain. This was deadly serious, and there was no turning back. She was in far too deep.

Because of the quasi lockdown, she was determined to make a lot of progress going through the electronic evidence records she had, including all the financials they had gathered so far in the investigation into Ana's businesses. If she couldn't work the cases on the ground, she could do what she did best—analyze evidence and make legal arguments to build a case.

Zach walked into the big living room that they had set up as a workroom with a large wooden table and multiple chairs. She sat there now and looked at him as he took a seat.

"How's it going?" he asked.

"I'm reviewing all the current financial records that we were able to obtain from the subpoena."

"I think I have some news that will make you happy."

She looked up at him. "What is it?"

"Two things actually. First, I know you wanted us to try to talk to the workers at the dry cleaner's. Obviously, you and I can't do that now. But I've talked to Brodie and we're going to send in a couple of undercover agents to sniff around and see if they can get any of Ana's employees talking."

"That is good news."

"And there's more." He pulled an envelope out of his pocket and handed it to her.

"What's this?"

"In there is another electronic file that was just dropped off here by one of our agents. I'm told it's a treasure trove of documents from our confidential informant."

Now that was something to get excited about. "I can't wait to review all the documents and see what kind of case we can really start building." She started putting together possible scenarios in her mind before she even popped the drive into the laptop to start looking.

"Any preliminary thoughts on charges?" he asked.

"Obviously the drug-trafficking charge would be huge if we could get enough evidence. If we have better evidence this time, then the same charges we brought against Simon could be brought against Ana with regard to the money laundering. But I need to be able to make the drug charges stick, or this case won't have real legs. I don't know if Ian would be on board with bringing another money laundering case so soon against the Hernandez family. If we go in, we want to bring something big to the table."

"Hit them with everything we have," Zach said.

"Yeah, but I don't want to jump to any conclusions about what will happen. Ideally, I'd like to examine all the evidence we have and then start making determinations about what type of charges are appropriate. We can't afford another not-guilty verdict. I know Ian doesn't want the prosecutor's office to look incompetent. It would be a bad reflection on me, of course, but also him and everyone else in the office. With Simon, at least we could provide the explanation about Denise's murder after the fact. But the public will expect something better from us next time."

"That makes total sense to me. You want to go out strong this time because last time you felt you were in an uphill battle."

"That's an understatement."

He reached out and touched her forearm. "How are you really doing, Jess?"

As she looked into his eyes she understood that he wanted to see how she was holding up. "I'm pushing through."

"You don't have to shoulder this by yourself. I'm here, too." He moved his hand down her arm and took her hand. "It hit me that you could've been killed, and I didn't really even know how to think about a world without you in it."

Her heart hurt hearing his tender words. Because deep down she was still worried that she may not be the woman that he needed. "Zach, I feel like you're putting me up on some pedestal, and I'm worried that I won't ever live up to your expectations."

"Why would you say something like that?" He squeezed her hand.

"Because I want you to be happy, and I'm not sure I'm capable of being the person to bring that to you. I don't know if you fully comprehend how deep my bruises go."

"I can't pretend to know what you went through as a child, but I can say that the woman who is sitting in front of me now isn't weak. She's a strong and independent person who is fulfilling her goals and not backing down to any threat—no matter how large."

"I may put on a brave face, but there are times when I am anything but."

"Jess, don't you realize that's just part of being human? We all have doubts and fears. Insecurities and hang-ups."

She shook her head. "Yes, but those feelings don't totally define most people. I sometimes feel trapped by everything that has happened to me. It's almost suffocating." She couldn't believe that she was baring her deepest fears and thoughts with this man. That scared her.

"I may be speaking out of turn here, but you're only trapped if you allow yourself to be."

She pulled her hand back from his. "You think I want to live like this?"

"I didn't mean it like that."

"What did you mean, then?"

"You're the only one who sees yourself as being weak. You're stronger than your past. You've overcome the struggles. Embrace that and look to living each day looking forward and not back."

"It's easy for someone to say that who hasn't lived my life. Who doesn't wake up many nights in a cold sweat and full of angst and fear."

He reached out and squeezed her hands again. "I care about you. More than you probably want me to." He paused. "You can start fresh right here and now."

"I want nothing more than that." She felt the tears pooling up in her eyes. She didn't understand what Zach really saw in her. But she couldn't deny that she felt something for him, too. Stronger feelings than anything she'd ever experienced in her life.

He let go of her and reached out to gently brush away the tear that had fallen down her cheek. "Jess, all I'm asking is for you to keep an open mind about the possibility of a future once this case is over. Just promise me you won't shut me out because I couldn't handle that."

"I don't want to shut you out. I'm just going to take it one day at a time."

"That's enough for me."

But would it be enough for her?

ELEVEN

Zach was a bit disturbed that he'd been summoned into the FBI field office. Was he in some sort of trouble? Was Ford going to remove him from the case because he'd taken Jessica out to do on-the-ground investigations of Ana's businesses? Or was there some other misstep that he wasn't even aware of?

Whatever it was, he was about to find out. He'd left Jessica with Brodie at the safe house and was about to walk into the meeting with the big boss man. It wasn't every day that a rookie FBI agent was called into a private meeting with the special agent in charge.

The fact that Brodie hadn't been included in the meeting did give him a shred of hope that he wouldn't be fired. Since Zach reported directly to Brodie, Zach assumed that Brodie would need to be in on any major decision that impacted his job, or at least that was Zach's hope.

"He's ready for you now, Agent Taylor." The dark-haired receptionist smiled and gave him a reassuring nod. He wondered if she did that to everyone, even if they were about to be fed to the wolves.

He took a deep breath, stood up straight and walked into Ford's office ready to face the music.

"Zach, come on in," Ford said. "Take a seat."

Ford got up from his desk and shut the door behind Zach. That couldn't be a good sign.

Zach did as he was directed and sat down. He waited for Ford to take his seat and start the meeting.

"You're probably wondering why I wanted to speak to you today," Ford said, his hazel eyes serious.

"Yes, sir. I'm anxious to hear what it is you'd like to discuss." Zach prayed that he wasn't about to get fired. He had so much more to do as an FBI agent. Yeah, he shouldn't have taken Jessica out of the safe house like that, but it wasn't a mistake he would repeat. And he was a stronger agent for it, having been tested.

"Well, first things first. Brodie briefed me on what happened and the close call you had with Jessica while the two of you were out working on the Ana Hernandez case."

"Yes, sir, about that. I should apologize. We were both anxious to get out there and do some actual investigatory work. But in retrospect, I never should've taken Jessica down there. At the time it seemed like a good idea, but I can clearly see now that it was a misjudgment, and I can assure you it won't happen again."

Ford lifted up his hand, and Zach immediately shut up.

"Actually, from what I hear from Brodie, you saved Jessica's life. If it hadn't been for you, that SUV would've run her over."

"Yes, but I put her in that situation to begin with, sir."

"Zach, this is your first assignment as an FBI agent out of Quantico. I don't expect you to make perfect decisions every day. You're not going to be judged against a guy who's been with the bureau twenty years. All I ask of you is that you do your best, use your best judgment and don't make the same mistake twice." He paused. "And you should know that you come highly recommended out of the Academy. I got a few personal phone calls about you when you first started, Zach. You have a raw talent that doesn't come along very often. You just need the right people guiding you. And Brodie is one of the best."

"Thank you, sir. I am trying to do the absolute best job that I can. I think our enthusiasm for the investigation just clouded my decision-making. But I've learned from that and will make sure next time I am more cautious, especially where Jessica is concerned. I realize that she isn't one of us and doesn't need to be treated as such."

"The last thing on this topic I'll say is that you are doing a fine job as a rookie agent. I remember being in your shoes, and it's much harder now than it was back when I came through. But having said all of that, that's not really the reason I wanted to speak with you today."

If it wasn't about what had just happened with Jessica, then what could Ford possibly want with him right now? Why not go to Brodie? Zach sat with his fists clenched in anticipation of what Ford was going to say.

"Anyway, there's something else." Ford looked him directly in the eyes. "I am going to be reassigning your priorities. Effective immediately, you are going to be working solely on matters related to the Luke Hernandez and Ivan Markov investigation. We're short on resources, and I need you focused on that case."

"Really?" He hadn't seen that coming.

"Yes," Ford said flatly.

"I understand, sir," he said. He didn't feel as though it was his place to challenge Ford.

"The Markov case has extreme interest all the way up to the highest levels of the bureau. Given the break we have with Luke, we can't mess this up. I've been told in no uncertain terms that the powers that be fully expect us to be able to gather the evidence and get arrests for both men."

"And the Ana Hernandez case?" Zach asked.

"It's placed on the back burner for now. We just had the big loss against Simon. The case against Ana is moving forward, but from everything I've heard, we're not in a position to be able to act right away. It's a no-brainer that we would shift priorities. Markov is huge. And you should see this as a big career opportunity for you. If you're involved in a takedown of this magnitude, then that will be a big résumé booster. Ana's not going anywhere. She can wait."

"And what about the prosecutor's office? Do you know if Jessica will be receiving the same message?"

Ford nodded. "I had a long talk with Ian this morning about both cases and all the facts and moving parts involved. He agrees that we need to focus on the biggest criminal threat first—and in this situation that is hands down Ivan Markov. There is no dispute about that. Add to that the potential of a corrupt police detective working for Markov and, well, I don't have to spell out all of those implications for you."

Zach leaned forward in his seat, engaged in the conversation. "No, you don't. I've had my suspicions about Luke from the start. Has there been any further development with tracking him down?"

Ford shook his head. "Unfortunately not. I'm a bit concerned that he may have gotten out of the country before our investigation even started. But we won't give up. We're going to run this thing all the way to the ground, including finding every other corrupt cop in the Miami PD that was in on this thing—if he was working with any other cops, that is. That's another reason it's so important for us to figure out how this scheme works. Is Luke working as a lone wolf with Markov or is there a complex web of corruption in the Miami PD? We can't let police corruption continue. The public demands more from them and from us."

"I understand, sir." Zach thought about Ford's words. If he was involved in a case of this magnitude and they took down a man like Markov, it would be an amazing start to his FBI career.

"I just wanted to make sure you were okay with this reassignment. I still want you working with Jessica, but only on the Luke Hernandez case."

"I'm hearing you loud and clear, sir."

"This could be a strategic move for us. Let the Hernandez family think that Jessica has shifted her efforts. Then maybe they'll lay off. Especially if Mick gets wind of what happened and becomes involved. Regardless, though, we can't assume that Mick controls any of his children. So you still need to be on high alert as far as Jessica's safety goes. And no more investigations related to Ana until we get this other case closed. Understood?"

"Absolutely."

"Good. Well, then get out of here and back to work. I'll be sending over some additional hard-copy files on the Luke case today for you and Jessica to work through. It's an extensive amount, but I figure between the two of you, that you'll be able to handle it. We're trying to do the deep dive on everything associated with Luke's life to connect all the dots to Markov."

"We'll get right on it." Zach stood up and walked out of Ford's office. It wasn't until he reached the elevator that he realized he'd been holding his breath. He hadn't known what to expect from the meeting, but all things considered, that had actually gone well.

He was going to be working the biggest case they had going, and he'd also still be teaming up with Jessica. He knew that her reaction probably wasn't going to be the same as his. While she definitely wanted to work on the Luke investigation, too, she wanted to follow through on Ana's. That would still be possible, but it would just have to wait. He figured he could help make her understand that the FBI had limited resources and had to go after the bigger fish in the sea first.

He arrived back at the safe house and found Jessica seated in front of her laptop in the kitchen.

"Where's Brodie?" he asked.

"He's in the family room watching TV."

He walked over closer to her. "Have you talked to Ian?"

She looked up from her computer. "No, why do you ask?"

"Because I have a feeling he's going to be contacting you soon."

"What happened at your meeting with Ford?"

He didn't know that it would be best for him to be the one to talk to her about this before she spoke to her boss. "Maybe you should call Ian first."

She stood up and walked over to where he stood. "No, Zach. Please tell me what's going on. I'd rather hear it from you."

"It's nothing bad." Well, he didn't think so, but she might.

She crossed her arms in front of her. "Then why do you have that concerned look on your face?"

"Because I think you might take the news a little differently than I did."

"C'mon, Zach. First you have to tell me what the news is."

"The FBI has decided to prioritize the investigation into Luke and Markov. From here on out, I'm only going to be working on that case. Not on Ana's case until further notice—likely not until after the Luke case gets put to bed."

"So you're saying that they told us not to work the Ana case anymore?"

"Ford told me that. When I asked if he had spoken to Ian about the prosecutorial side, he indicated that he had and that Ian agreed that the two of us should keep working together but focus our efforts on just that one case."

She let out a sigh. "Is this because of what we did going after Ana's businesses and the SUV coming after us?"

"No. I don't think so, but I think that's a side benefit to us shifting priorities. I think Ford is a bit uncomfortable with having you being active in the field, especially given the unknown threat level against you. This way we're working on the case that matters most, and you'll be safer being out of the spotlight from the Hernandez family."

She grabbed his hand. "And how do you feel about this?"

"I'm actually excited about getting more involved with the bigger case. But I didn't want you to be disappointed. I know you had your sights set on Ana. And it's my understanding that they still want to go after her. Just not right now. It just means us waiting."

"And by then Ana could have made major moves to build up her criminal empire while we were sitting back and doing nothing. This is exactly what Mick Hernandez wanted. We're playing right into his hands. Don't you see that?"

"But we're not sitting back. We're working one of the top cases of the FBI. That's huge, Jess."

She put her hands on her hips. "So this is about career advancement for you?"

"And yours, too. I wouldn't take this as a negative. We could do some great work here. Ian's having some files sent over related to Luke today. He wants us to do the deep dive into his life."

"But what about doing the right thing? Isn't the right thing to go after both of them?"

He nodded. "And we will. It's a matter of timing. I didn't get the impression that the FBI wanted to can the Ana investigation. Just that this Luke thing is so much more important and the connection to Markov has everyone's hair on fire. Ford said the interest in Luke's case goes all the way up to the top of the FBI."

She nodded. "I guess you're right. I can totally see the FBI perspective here. I just hate leaving things unfinished."

"We'll come back to it when the time is right. But for now, we need to move full speed ahead with the other investigation. This is an opportunity for us to play a key role on the evidentiary investigation and make a difference in this case."

"What are we going to be looking for in the documents that are being sent over?"

"Connections between anything and everything in Luke's life and Ivan Markov or his known associates. Ford wants to be able to build a rock-solid case."

"Okay. I'm in."

Jessica and Zach had multiple laptops open on the table in the workroom at the safe house. The FBI had a vendor print out thousands of pages of electronic evidence for them to review. Plus they had multiple electronic files to go over. The task was a bit daunting, but Jessica had felt a wave of adrenaline kick in when the banker boxes of documents had started to arrive.

Zach was right. This was big, and she should want

to be a part of it. What if she found the smoking gun? She had to be careful to balance her career agenda with the larger goal at hand—finding the truth and apprehending those that are guilty. But she was determined to figure out what was going on here.

"How's your stack going so far?" Zach asked. He had a huge pile of documents in front of him that he appeared to have cut in about half from the time he started.

"Nothing that interesting so far. The financial records I'm reviewing look pretty standard. Luke wasn't living a fancy lifestyle by any stretch of the imagination. You would think that if he was dirty, he would at least indulge in some expensive purchases."

"Yeah, but remember, we're looking at everything. Just because one account comes up clean doesn't mean Luke is clean. We have to analyze each one of the accounts."

She smiled. "Zach, you convicted Luke from day one. You and I both know that. You didn't even need any physical evidence to form your opinion."

"Okay, I'll give that point to you. I have never trusted that man. But you can't deny the evidence that Mick brought to you. We've run down everything and concluded that there's no way that Luke was working with any sanctioned government operation. So you give me a plausible explanation for those pictures."

As he challenged her, she readied her comeback. "I don't have a good explanation at this point. I just hate to believe that I could've been wrong about him." One thing she felt good about was her ability to determine people's true intentions. That's a big reason this whole thing bothered her. If she was wrong about Luke, what else was she wrong about in her life?

"Even the best and most highly trained FBI agents get it wrong sometime. That's the thing about skilled criminals—they are like chameleons, able to blend in and make you think they're something they're not. And you have to admit, Luke learned from the best. His entire family is full of criminals. Even if he wanted to do the right thing, I imagine it was hard to see his family in a life of crime and living the high life while he was living on a cop salary barely scraping by."

"But do you really believe that? He had the courage to step out of that life. To make his own way independent of his family, and do it at much personal danger and risk to himself. I find it hard to swallow that Luke's that motivated by money."

He laughed. "Jess, I think most people are motivated by money."

"Are you?" she challenged.

"No, and you aren't, either, but I think we are in the minority on that."

She agreed with him and decided to let the discussion go right now. They continued to review the documents. A couple of hours went by, and Jessica realized this was going to take much longer than she'd thought. As she flipped through another stack of papers, she had to do a double take. She looked at the document closely before she said anything. She wanted to be sure of what she was seeing. After a couple of minutes, she needed another set of eyes. "Hey, Zach. Come and take a look at this." She took the piece of paper she was analyzing and put it in front of him.

"Something is off here," she said.

"How so?"

She pointed to the document. "I was cross-referencing this bank statement against the spreadsheet and support-ing documentation that Mick provided. Look here." She pulled the printed version of the spreadsheet out of an-other pile and put it beside the bank statement. "In the spreadsheet that reflects the banking records, it shows that there was a large deposit into Luke's bank account that then got wired to an offshore bank account. But in the original bank statement there's absolutely no record of that deposit."

"Let me look at this," Zach said. He put both docu-ments in front of him and stared at them in silence for a minute. "Something doesn't match up here."

"Exactly. They can't both be right."

Zach ran his hand through his hair. "We need to look at that spreadsheet and cross-reference every entry and the supporting documents that were provided by Mick against the originals we now have in front of us."

Three hours later and they'd gone through the exer-cise. But every other document matched up exactly as it should have. "I'm sorry, Zach, but doesn't this seem strange?"

"Yes. But there could be an explanation."

"Like someone edited these documents to make Luke look guilty."

"That's a stretch—don't you think?" he asked.

"I'm not willing to rule anything out at this point."

"It's one discrepancy," he said.

"Yes, but that still means that someone had to have changed the documentation that Mick provided to us."

Her phone rang, and she picked it up.

"Ms. Hughes," Mick said.

"Mr. Hernandez." She knew exactly who it was and flipped it to speaker so Zach could hear.

"I understand that you didn't heed my warning from our nice meeting at the Bay Café and were out and about poking around my daughter's businesses."

"And did you also hear that I was almost run down in the process?"

"I can't say that I heard anything like that specifically. But this is a courtesy call to remind you of what you should be focusing on and that you need to be extra cautious these days."

"I don't like being threatened, Mr. Hernandez. I have a job to do. And if you come after me, I won't be conducting any investigation of any sort against anyone."

"Well, the problem is this. You know how children are. They don't always listen to their parents. And you're not making it very easy on me—as you know I can't tell them what I told you. So it would be best for you to focus on the matter we discussed. I can't make any other guarantees about your safety."

The line went dead. She looked over at Zach. "What do you make of that?"

"Sounds like he's trying to tell you that his kids are still after you. He put himself in a strange position because he can't exactly tell them to lay off or they would want to know why. Since he's trying to keep this Luke thing on the down low, it means that you're still a target regardless of who or what you're investigating."

"We're here at the safe house. I don't have anything to worry about right now. Especially since we've been cut off from the Ana investigation."

"And all the more reason to lay low and focus on the work that we can do from here. We still have tons of documents to analyze. I'll put in a call to Brodie to let him know about the discrepancies in the financial records. I'm sure he'll want to look at what you discovered right away. I'll also let him know that you had contact from Mick."

"Sounds good." But as she looked down at the documents in front of her, she couldn't shake the feeling that something was off.

Jessica was having another vivid nightmare. Her attacker was strong—much stronger than her and she felt powerless to fight back. Why wasn't she fighting back? She sucked in a breath of air and then woke with a start.

That's when she realized she wasn't dreaming. No, this was all too real. A man had his strong hands on her, and he was pulling her up out of the bed and onto her feet, dragging her across the bedroom.

Quickly processing what was happening, she let out a scream. The assailant tried to cover her mouth, but she bit down hard. He let out a foul curse, but she didn't back down as she struggled against him. There was no way she was giving up and letting this man take her away to what would surely be certain death.

Lord, please give me strength.

How had someone gotten into the safe house? Now wasn't the time to ask questions as she tried to fight off the intruder. She let out another bloodcurdling scream, hoping that Zach would hear and would come to her aid. In the meantime, she would use the skills she'd learned and do everything she could to at least try to neutralize her attacker.

He pushed her toward the window, and it occurred to her that he might try to throw her through the glass. Her bedroom was on the second floor. If he did, it could be a fatal fall.

It was at that point that she really regretted Zach taking the downstairs bedroom so that she would have more privacy. She wondered if he could even hear her screams.

The man pushed her hard, but she was able to maintain her footing. She delivered a hard kick to his abdomen that made him stagger backward. Now wasn't the time to keep trying to fight him off. She started to run, and she screamed Zach's name as loud as she could as she tore down the hallway and down the stairs.

By the time she reached the bottom of the stairs, Zach was racing toward her with his weapon drawn.

"There's a man in my room," she said.

"Stay here," he said. He ran up the stairs, and she waited at the bottom, trying to catch her breath. She realized she was shaking and tried to calm down.

A couple of minutes later, Zach rushed back down the steps. "He must have crawled out one of the windows. No one is up there now. I cleared every room."

She'd been as brave as she could, but she felt herself

near the breaking point as Zach's arms wrapped tightly around her. She drew strength and comfort from his warm embrace.

"I screamed, but you didn't hear me," she said.

"I am so sorry. The first time I heard you scream, I came running. How badly are you hurt?" He released her from the hug and looked down at her.

"More scared than hurt. I'm sure I'll be a little bruised, but, believe me, I've had to deal with much worse."

"Come on into the kitchen and have a seat. I'll get you something to drink, and you can tell me what happened." Gently he took her hand and led her to the table.

After she had a few sips of hot tea and had tried to calm herself down, she looked into Zach's dark eyes. "It was another nightmare. Or so I thought. When I woke up, the man was pulling me out of the bed. He was really strong."

"Did you see him? Can you describe him?"

"It was dark. And he had on some sort of mask so I couldn't see his face. But he was over six feet tall and very strong. I don't think it was the same man who attacked me in the parking lot. I believe this guy was a little bit taller. But I can't say for sure."

"That's okay. Just take your time and tell me what else happened."

"I screamed. I bit down on his hand as hard as I could. And I got in a few kicks. He was pushing me toward the window. I thought he might try to throw me out. I wasn't sure if I would survive that or not, or whether that was his ultimate plan. When I got one solid kick in that threw him off balance, that's when I started running down the steps."

"Okay. Take a minute while I make some calls. I have the feeling that we're going to be moving safe houses right away."

"As in tonight?" She looked over at the clock in the kitchen and saw it was about two-thirty in the morning.

"Yeah. This position has obviously been compromised. We can't take any further chances." Zach stepped into the next room to place the calls, giving her a moment alone.

Jessica sat drinking her tea and trying to pull herself together. This last attack had rattled her even more. There had been so much physical contact. It was like she was reliving the worst aspects of her past. The only difference is that this time she didn't just take it. She fought back.

Now was not the time to lose it. She had to pull it together. Zach was right there in the next room. She was safe. Nothing was going to happen to her. She kept reminding herself that she was no longer a defenseless child or teenager. She was a grown woman who wouldn't back down even in the midst of an attack.

Zach walked back into the kitchen with a frown on his face. "Jess, can you pack up what you need? I'd like to be on the road as soon as we can."

"Sure." She stood up from kitchen table.

Zach gently took her hand. "And I know you like your space, but from now on, I've got to stick a lot closer."

"I'd actually appreciate that." Right now she needed Zach by her side.

* * *

Zach kept his eyes focused on the road in front of him but checked the rearview mirror often. Jessica had barely spoken a word since they'd gotten in the car. And he couldn't shake the feeling that something was off about this entire situation.

Brodie had tried to calm him down on the phone, but Zach was amped up. But he didn't want Jessica to realize that he was so concerned. She'd already been through enough, especially with the latest assault. He couldn't believe that he hadn't heard her screams. He should've stayed in an upstairs bedroom. Yet another mistake he'd learn from, but it could've been a deadly one. If Jessica hadn't fought back. If she hadn't been trained in self-defense. Thank the Lord that she was okay. And he'd meant what he told her. She basically wasn't going to leave his sight.

Right now he was about to make a decision. One that could end up getting him fired. But he also had thought about it nonstop since the attack, and now he should let Jessica know his plans. It wasn't fair of him to operate without her input.

"Jess," he said. "You up?"

"Wide-awake," she responded.

"I need to talk to you about something."

"Why do I get the feeling that this is going to be even more bad news?"

"It's not like that." He took a breath, wondering how best to explain his thought process to her. "The FBI has provided us a new safe house."

"I get that. I assumed that's where we're going now."

"It's where we were told to go. But I'm having second thoughts." He put it out there.

"What do you mean?"

"I'm concerned that the system has been compromised in some way. Either an actual person at the FBI working against us or some electronic tampering. Regardless, I don't feel safe taking you to another FBI-sanctioned safe house because I fear that your location could be discovered."

"But then where are you going to take me?"

"I haven't decided yet. Right now I'm just driving around trying to figure out how to tell you about my plan. If you really want to go to an FBI safe house, then I will take you. I don't want you to do something you're not comfortable with."

"But you think that's not the best move?" she asked, her voice calm and even.

"I don't. How did the intruder find us? That's what I keep asking myself. The most plausible answers would lead one to conclude that there has been some type of security breach."

"What did you tell Brodie?"

"He thinks I'm taking you to the new sanctioned place. That's what he told me to do. That it was the best plan of action. But I'm worried that it's actually not safe."

She was silent for a minute before responding. "I agree with you. I've been sensing that something was off. And why take the risk? But where does this leave us with the FBI?"

"That's the thorny part. We'd basically be going off the grid. And I would need to get a new car because this one belongs to the bureau and it can be tracked."

"Do you feel like there's anyone you can trust right now?"

"It's not that I don't trust the FBI—it's that I worry that somehow the system has been infiltrated. And if the system is compromised, then that's going to be a problem for us. We can't get a rental because if someone is looking, they'll be able to track it back to us."

"Are there any other options?"

"I have an old college buddy who is deployed right now. He lives about a half an hour from here. I check on his house about once a month. He has a car, and he left me the keys. I know he wouldn't mind us using it. That's my best option. We'll get his vehicle, you'll drive it and I'll follow you. Then we'll ditch my car somewhere along the way and keep going."

"It's a plan."

"And, Jess, I could be completely wrong about all of this. If I am, I might lose my job, and we might be going on a total wild-goose chase."

"But if you're right, you just might be saving my life. Again."

They'd done just as Zach described with the pickup and exchange of vehicles. Now they were together in his friend's car and headed north. Even given the circumstances, Jessica was feeling better knowing that they had a game plan that didn't include anyone else.

She was with the only person she truly trusted. Yeah, he might have faith in all the agents at the FBI, but Jessica knew better. Anything was possible. It appeared that there could be corruption on so many different fronts that Jessica didn't even know where to begin.

"We'll stop soon and find a hotel. We'll get adjoining rooms and try to get a little rest before we make our next move."

"Who do you think sent the man that attacked me tonight?"

"It would be obvious to say that it was from the Hernandez family. Mick had just said that he couldn't control his kids. So that's an easy explanation. Ana got mad that you're coming after her. When the SUV couldn't take you out, she decided to get more aggressive."

"You don't sound convinced."

"Because what if we're missing something? What if there are other threats out there?"

"So you're thinking that the breach at the FBI didn't have to do with the Hernandez family, but something else?" she asked.

"I don't know. We can't rule out the possibility that somehow your connection to this Markov investigation was uncovered if there was a security breach at the FBI. And from everything I know about Markov, he's even more ruthless than Mick. I know that's hard to believe, but it's true."

"You didn't mention before that you thought I could be a target for Markov."

"I wanted to make sure we had things under control before I brought it up. I know it's a lot to take in,

Jess. And once again, maybe this is the rookie side of me wanting to make sure I'm not missing any possible threat. Regardless of where the threat is coming from, I'm not going to leave you."

"I know that, Zach. And I will vouch for you to Brodie, Ford and whoever else at the FBI might question what you've done here tonight."

"Ford told me to do everything in my power to keep you safe. And that's exactly what I'm trying to do. Since we trashed our phones, we'll have to get new ones today when the stores open."

"What will Brodie think happened to us? Won't he be worried?" she asked.

"Yes, but it's a small price to pay for your safety. He's a seasoned agent. He may figure out that I thought something was wrong and decided I had to act."

A thought occurred to her. "What if we're playing right into the enemy's hands?"

"What makes you ask that?"

"What if the whole point of whoever is behind this is that they wanted us out of the picture? To be on the run and afraid instead of investigating these cases."

"I hadn't considered that exact angle of having you stop your work. I've been so focused on your safety that I wasn't thinking of it in that way." He paused. "That opens up other possibilities related to the two investigations."

"Which makes me wonder if running away is the right thing to do." She'd come this far. It felt wrong to give up now.

"Here's a place we can stop and rest for a while. We'll discuss after we get some rest."

"Okay." But she already thought she had her answer. They needed to go back and finish what they'd started.

TWELVE

Wide-awake after having slept for about an hour, Jessica now found herself at the small desk in the hotel room. Zach was probably still asleep next door, and she didn't want to disturb him. He needed rest to be able to do his job. She, on the other hand, had nothing but nightmares the longer she lay in bed. It was better for her to stay awake. At least that way she could face her fears head-on.

So she sat there thinking about their situation. And praying for guidance. Because she really felt as though she needed God's help right now. She didn't want to put herself—or Zach—in unnecessary danger, but she also wanted to see this thing through.

Her thoughts were interrupted by a light tap on the hotel room door. Would Zach be coming to the main door? She figured he would've knocked on the adjoining.

She walked over to the door and looked through the peephole to ensure it was Zach before she opened it. She sucked in a breath.

On the other side of the door stood Luke Hernandez.

"Jessica," he said softly. "I know you're in there. Please let me in. I promise I'm not here to hurt you. But you're in danger. I'm still one of the good guys."

She had to make a decision. There was something deep inside her that told her to believe Luke. So she opened the door, and he walked into the room.

"Zach is right next door. He'll be in here in half a second if I yell."

He took a step toward her but held up his hands. "I told you, Jessica. I'm not here to hurt you. I'm not the one you should be afraid of."

"What's going on, Luke? How did you find us?"

"I tailed you all the way here once you left the safe house."

"But I never noticed anyone."

"Well, I am a trained law enforcement officer," he responded. Then he took a seat in one of the two chairs in her room.

She sat in the other. "What's going on with you and Ivan Markov?"

"That's one of the reasons I had to find you and Zach. I couldn't trust anyone else at this point." He paused. "I've been set up, Jessica."

"By who?"

"I don't know exactly. But it was someone in law enforcement. It has to be. No one else would have the skills—or the inside scoop—to pull off something like this."

She really wanted to believe him, but she needed to confront him directly and see how he responded. "Luke, I saw the photos of you and Markov."

Luke nodded. "I know. The photos are legitimate. I met with Markov."

"But why would you have done that?"

"Because I was assigned to."

"By who?"

"My boss at Miami PD told me I was working on a special highly confidential assignment. I believed him."

She took in what he was telling her and started to try to play it out. "Whoever is pulling the strings has people in multiple places working for him."

"So you believe me?" Luke asked, his dark eyes wide.

"I actually do. I never thought you were one of the bad guys. And then when I saw you had a discrepancy in your financial records that didn't match up with the evidence your father turned over to me, I thought something didn't add up."

"Wait." Luke leaned toward her. "My dad is involved in all of this?"

"Yes."

"How?"

"He actually called and asked for a meeting with me. He told me to lay off your sister and that he had evidence that you were involved in an illegal drug operation with other cops. He gave me a jump drive full of documents. But when I reviewed it, I didn't see anything about any other cops. But I did find a lot tying you to Ivan Markov."

Luke shook his head. "It was all a setup. I had no idea my father was involved. This is making more sense, though."

"That your father would be involved?"

"My father has been trying to take out Markov for about three years. But it's much harder than you would think. Even for someone like Mick Hernandez."

"And what about you?" she asked. "Did you know that your father was targeting you?"

Luke let out a big breath. "I knew that he wasn't happy with me. He wanted me to help Simon, but I told him there wasn't anything I could do. I went to the trial, but it wasn't because I believed that Simon was innocent. I know my dad has a pretty big evil streak, but even I didn't think he would come at me directly like that. Although come to think of it, I was probably just collateral damage or icing on the cake. He cares much more about Markov than he'll ever care about me. I can tell you that much. He might have seen an opportunity to deal with me at the same time as taking down his nemesis."

Her head was swimming with all of this information. And the fact that Luke was sitting directly in front of her. And not as a threat—as a friend. "Who do you think is coming after me?"

"I wouldn't put it past my father to play both sides. But you know what? Whoever set me up may be after you, too. You said you found some evidentiary discrepancies?"

"Only one. Everything else was airtight. But Zach did report what we found up the chain."

Luke nodded. "Which means if he reported it up, then everyone that matters would know about it by now, including those we wouldn't want to know. I don't know who we can trust."

"This is a tangled web. We don't know who is working with who or what the final agenda is. And most importantly, who is the one in charge and calling the shots?"

"We do know that my father is after me, and would probably be happy if you were out of the picture, too. Especially since he thinks you're going to go after Ana. She's his pride and joy. Let me tell you, Simon has issues, but Ana is our father through and through. A combination of smart, deadly and depraved. I wouldn't put anything past her."

"But your father is the one who came to me and asked me to prosecute you. I assume he wanted me alive to be able to carry that through."

"Yeah, but he's a smart man. He knows that you wouldn't bring a case unless you were certain. And since it's a setup, he'd have to know the likelihood of it all coming together is slim. But it got you off Ana's case for a bit and put the heat on Markov."

"Which would allow Mick and Ana to do something big while everyone's attention was on you and Markov. Sounds like a pretty brilliant plan. Especially if it ended with your father's competition being put away after all these years."

A loud knock sounded at the adjoining door.

"Uh-oh. That's Zach. You might want to be careful because when I let him in, he's going to freak out that you're here."

"Understood," Luke said.

Slowly Jessica opened the door, and Zach walked in. "I thought I heard voices."

Zach's eyes locked on to Luke's. Without hesitation, Zach pulled his weapon.

"Put the gun down, Zach. It's okay," she said. Then she reached out and touched his arm that wasn't holding the gun.

"What are you doing here?" Zach asked Luke.

"It's a long story," Luke responded. "But the short version is that once I realized I was being set up, I went dark. Trying to figure out who framed me. And I needed to let you guys know the truth."

"How can you claim that?" Zach asked loudly. "I saw the photos of you and Markov together. The FBI determined they weren't doctored. So you better come up with a more convincing story."

"Zach, let the man speak," Jessica urged. "We all need to be on the same page here. And it would help if you lowered your gun."

"First, tell me where your firearm is, Luke. I want to see it. Put it on the ground, slowly."

Luke did as Zach asked and removed his gun from his waistband, placing it on the hotel room floor. "See?" He held up both of his hands. "I'm not a threat to the two of you. I'm one of the good guys."

"Explain yourself," Zach ordered.

"As I told Jessica, I was told by my supervisor at Miami PD that I was going to be assigned to work on an undercover sting that was a joint agency operation. DEA, FBI, Miami PD, the whole nine yards. The op required me to meet Markov. I was tasked with playing the role of dirty cop who wanted to get in with his business. And that's exactly what I did. What I didn't know until just now when I spoke with Jessica is that my father had some role in all of this."

"And we don't know who actually set Luke up to take the fall," she added.

"Right," Luke said. "All my orders came straight through my boss, Steve Young. I don't know whether he was in on it or if they tricked him into thinking it was a legitimate operation and he was just executing what he thought was all aboveboard."

"But he and everyone else denied there being any undercover operation." Zach started pacing back and forth in the hotel room while Luke didn't say a word.

Jessica was still trying to process the whole thing. After a few minutes of silence, she decided to speak up. "I think we should go back and face this down. Figure out what Ana is really up to with Mick and also determine who is working with Mick to set up Luke. It has to be someone on the inside of law enforcement. This is far too big to just walk away from. We can't risk it getting even bigger than what it is now, and we don't know how far the corruption goes."

Zach immediately started shaking his head. "That's way too dangerous, Jessica. We know that you're a target. Why would I take you back into that?"

"Because it's the only way that I'll ever be safe again. We need to get to the bottom of this. Ferret out the true criminals here. If not, I could be looking over my shoulder the rest of my life. That isn't how I want to live."

"She's right, you know," Luke said. "If we walk away from this now, we'll still be at risk."

Zach turned his attention to Luke. "Man, I still haven't bought everything you've said. You're treading on really thin ice right now."

Jessica appreciated that Zach was trying to protect her, but he needed to be more objective. She needed to try to defuse the situation right now. "Luke, will you excuse us for one moment? I'd like to speak to Zach."

"Sure," Luke said. "Go ahead. I'll just wait right here."

Jessica grabbed Zach's hand and led him into his room, shutting the adjoining door behind them. Then she walked over to him and looked directly into his eyes. "Zach, I am thankful for how much you are trying to keep me safe. And the level of dedication you have to my security. But you've got to be a bit more open-minded about Luke."

Zach reached up and gently touched her cheek. "Can't you see, Jessica? I'm willing to do anything in this world to keep you out of danger. I can't afford to trust anyone where your safety is concerned. Because honestly I don't know how I'd be able to make it if something happened to you—especially on my watch."

"And that means the world to me, but I'm telling you that Luke isn't one of the men we need to be concerned about. He's on the run, too. His father is trying to take him out, and who knows what other enemies he has? At this point, we should see him as an ally, not an enemy."

"How can you be so sure?" he asked.

"When I look in his eyes, I believe he's telling me the

truth. And beyond that, his story makes a whole lot of sense when you look at all the facts. The discrepancy I found in the documents. Mick's level of involvement. I find it totally plausible that Luke felt he was doing his job when he was working with Markov. So I'm asking you if we can go back in there and if you will give him a chance."

Zach didn't immediately respond. Then he nodded his head. "I'd do anything for you, Jess."

Her heart pounded at his words, but now wasn't the time to focus on her romantic feelings. "Thanks, Zach. Let's go."

They walked back into her room and found Luke seated in one of the chairs.

"Okay," Zach said. "Where were we?"

"I understand that you would be hesitant about all of this," Luke said. "And about me in general. But think about it. If I'd wanted to hurt Jessica, she'd be dead by now. That wasn't my intention and never will be. I know you find it hard to believe that anything good could ever come out of my family, but I refuse to be defined by them. I made a choice to take a different path—a much harder path. One not filled with luxuries and people doing whatever I tell them. But I still have my soul and my integrity—and a strong faith in God that has gotten me through all of these incredibly tough times. So I hope that you would look at me now, man to man, and realize that I'm telling the truth. That I'm here to help and not hurt."

Hearing Luke's impassioned words rendered her speechless. But what was even more stunning was watching Zach's reaction. Zach walked over to Luke and offered him his hand. The handshake between the two men solidified an alliance and what Jessica hoped would be friendship. They were going to need to work together if they were going to get out of this mess.

"Okay, guys," she said. "Now that we're on the same page, we need to come up with a plan."

"Jessica's right," Luke said. "There are so many moving parts here."

"The way I see it, we have a couple of issues to tackle," Zach said. "We need to determine what Ana is planning. We had intel that something big was going to go down. What if the timing of that got pushed back and it's still to come? With us out of the picture, that would open up a way for them to operate unfettered."

"And two," Jessica said. "We need to determine who is setting up Luke to take this fall for the Markov operation."

"What's your relationship like with Markov?" Zach asked Luke.

"It's good, but it was a ruse. He thinks I'm one of the bad guys. My cover story was bolstered by the fact that I could say that I wanted to work with him not only because of the size of money involved with his drug operation but because it was personal, a way to get back at my father."

"Maybe we can use your Markov connection in our favor," Jessica said. "I'm just thinking out loud here, guys. I'm sure Markov has sources everywhere. What if we can get intel from him about what Ana is really up to? Markov could provide us absolutely vital information on what her intentions are and probably operational details, as well. We go after her and shut down whatever they have going and gain evidence to be able to put on a case against Ana. Then we also have to work our own sources to determine who could be after you, Luke. We could go back and act like we never saw you. Go about our business while you work the Markov angle and report back to us."

"I'll still have to operate in the shadows and try to meet Markov in private locations. I'll need your help to run down certain leads I uncover," Luke said. "There's no one I can trust in Miami PD or the FBI. Everyone either thinks I'm guilty or could possibly be in on it."

"I know this won't be a popular thing to say," Zach put in. "But I'm still worried about the threats to Jessica in all of this. She isn't a member of law enforcement. And we're talking tactical operations here that shouldn't involve a lawyer."

"But I can handle it, Zach," she told him. "I'm not afraid." And that was true. She felt less fear than she had in years.

Zach walked over to her. "Jess, you're a tough woman, but I can't let you just walk back into an open area with multiple targets on your back yelling 'come and get me.' We have to be smart about this."

"I can handle this, Zach. I know it's your job to protect me, but we can't just sit back while all of this implodes and try to clean up the mess after the fact."

"I understand that. But if there's ever a choice between any of this work and your safety, you know what my position is going to be. You will always come first."

THIRTEEN

As Zach and Jessica settled into the FBI safe house they were originally assigned to, Zach realized that he would have to explain his brief absence of contact to his superiors.

So when Brodie showed up not long after Zach contacted him, Zach knew he was going to be in hot water. But he was more than ready to face whatever tongue-lashing was in store. He was going to be up front. He had felt it wasn't safe and had done what he thought he had to do.

"What in the world happened to you?" Brodie asked. They sat at the kitchen table by themselves.

"After Jessica was attacked at the last safe house, I reacted on instinct. I know you said we had this secure location available, but seeing her afraid, and me being caught off guard like that... Brodie—the intruder was able to break in. He got into Jessica's room and attacked her. I felt like the best thing to do—the only thing to do—was to take her somewhere no one knew about."

"Then why did you come back?"

"Because I realized ultimately we are safer working within the FBI structure. There are other resources that we can use. If we go it alone, we wouldn't have that."

Brodie nodded. "Zach, you have a lot of potential as an agent. And I don't want this one rash decision to cause you any problems. So here's what I'm going to do. I'm not going to tell Ford about this. He has enough on his plate right now without worrying about you going rogue."

"Thank you, Brodie." Zach let out a sigh of relief. He didn't need any more problems.

"But let me make sure you understand one thing very clearly. You can't do what you did last night. We are a team and we work together for the goal we're trying to accomplish. Including keeping Jessica safe. Do you understand?"

"Yes, sir. I do."

"Good. I trust I don't have to stay here and babysit you and can get out of here and keep working on tracking down Luke Hernandez. Here's a new FBI phone since I know you ditched your old one."

A slight thread of guilt went through Zach as he sat and looked into his boss's eyes. But he absolutely couldn't take the risk of telling Brodie that they had actually seen Luke. That there was something much more sinister going on here. He would just have to wait and deal with the consequences later.

"Thanks for everything, Brodie."

Brodie rose up from the kitchen table. "Make sure you stay in touch."

When he was alone again Zach took a few breaths.

God, am I doing the right thing? He took a moment and prayed for guidance. That he was placing his trust in the right people. Because what if Luke was playing him? What if he was putting Jessica in danger?

He pushed those doubts out of his mind—he needed to stay strong. They'd picked up burner phones that they would use to stay in touch with Luke. He was hoping that Luke was going to be able to meet up with Markov that afternoon—or at the latest by nighttime.

Jessica walked into the kitchen and took a seat beside him. "How're you doing?" she asked.

"Isn't that what I should be asking you?"

"We're a team, remember?"

"I'm ready to put an end to this. To catch Ana in a situation where there's no way out. And to find out who is behind this whole thing with Luke." He couldn't stop from reaching out and taking her hands. "Jess, can I ask you something?"

"Sure."

"When this is all over, where do you see us going?"

A slight frown pulled down at her lips. "I'm glad you brought that up because I've been thinking about it."

He didn't like the expression on her face. "I thought we were starting to build something here." He let go of her hands.

"I feel like that's partially my fault. I've been living in a fairy-tale world. Thinking I could just pick up and move on like a regular person without all the baggage of my past. But the more I think about it, the more I realize that I don't know how that will be possible. And before you try to say otherwise, I know that you think I can push through all of this, and I held out hope that I could, too. But I feel like in the end, all I'd ever bring you is pain and the inability to give myself fully to you—to anyone. And I do care about you so very much. I don't want to hurt you."

Now he was totally regretting having started this conversation. He believed she was acting out of fear. But he wasn't going to push it. They were both under a lot of stress. It was better to let it go and revisit it after they'd gotten through this ordeal. "Why don't we talk about this later?"

She didn't fight him and instead just nodded her head. "So what's our next move?"

"We wait for Luke to contact us. Hopefully he will have info we can use against Ana."

"Maybe in the meantime you can try to catch a nap. I know you didn't get much sleep when we stopped at the hotel."

She was right. He was exhausted even though he didn't want to admit it. Although it was largely from the stress of everything. "If you'll be okay, maybe I will lie down for a little bit. Maybe you should rest, too. Tonight could be a big night."

"Let's hope it is."

Jessica had tried to take a nap and had gotten about two hours of pretty decent sleep. Zach had been out for about four hours. And she had let him rest. It had broken her heart to push Zach away. She didn't think there was a feasible alternative. Because the last thing she wanted in the world was to hurt him, and inside she still felt so broken.

When her burner phone rang, her heart jumped. She picked it up, knowing that only one person could be calling.

"Hello," she said.

"Hey, it's Luke."

"Are you all right?"

"Yes. And I have big news. Is Zach around?"

"Yes, he was just taking a nap. Do you want me to get him?"

"Yeah, this is important. And we need to act on this intel."

"One second." She walked up the stairs to get him just as Zach walked out of the room where he'd been resting. His dark hair was tousled, and he'd never looked more handsome than at that moment. But she couldn't afford to be distracted right now.

"What's happening?" Zach asked.

"I've got Luke on the line." She put the phone on Speaker. They walked into the den and took a seat.

Zach's eyes lit up. "Luke, what do you have?"

"Big news, guys. Big news."

"What happened?" Jessica asked.

"So I had the meeting about an hour ago. I laid out the bait. Said that I wanted to take Ana out for him as a way to get back at my family. He was more than happy to have me do his dirty work. And I think that he believes I might actually kill my sister. But he also put on the table that if his intel was good, we could lead the cops right to her."

"Where? And what intel?" Zach asked.

"Here's the story. Ana is supposed to be receiving a huge shipment tonight. The drugs are going to be stored on her personal yacht. Markov's people have heard that she has custom-built areas of the yacht to store the product. So in an ideal world, we'd be able to catch her as she was transporting the drugs onto her yacht. It's her property and given the sensitivity of this operation, she is going to be there to oversee it."

"And what does Markov think about all of this?" Jessica asked.

"He's furious that she thinks she can invade his turf. For years, my family's illegal endeavors included many different things, but they have never been major players in the drug distribution business. Markov sees this as a direct frontal attack by the Hernandez family against his empire. Frankly, I fear that if we don't get to Ana first and get her into police custody, it's only a matter of time before Markov's men literally take her out. As much as I disagree with my sister's life of crime, I certainly don't want anything to happen to her. I believe there's always a chance at redemption."

"We need to think this through," Zach said. He looked down at his watch. "It's seven o'clock now. When do we think the shipment was going to happen?"

"Certainly after dark. But Markov could only tell me that it was happening tonight."

"We need to be down there. How do we think this transfer is going to happen from the original shipment?"

"If I were going to do it, I'd hand over the product off

the large freight ship into smaller boats and then have those go to the yacht."

"We need to get to that yacht," Jessica said. "Where does your sister keep it?"

"I can do even better. One of Markov's people put a GPS tracking device on her boat when word of this first hit. And I've got it in my possession. We'll be able to get right to her. But I think it makes sense for us to split up. You two go to the yacht. I'll be at the original shipment drop off point at the pier. You should use my boat. It's down at the harbor. Because we can't assume that the transfer is going to happen while they are docked."

"Good point," Zach said.

"Okay, now that I'm thinking this through. Let's meet at my boat. I will give you the keys. The only way this will work is if you're in the water and are able to actually catch her in the act. Then I'll station myself at the marina where the shipment is to come in. We'll stay in contact each step of the way. I'll bring some special night-vision equipment I have with me, too, so that you can try to document the transfer."

"Sounds good," Zach said. "Send me the location of your boat. We'll meet you there in an hour."

"See you then," Luke said.

Jessica ended the call and looked at Zach. "How are we feeling about this?" she asked.

"This could be huge. But I'm a little concerned that we aren't looping in the FBI. If we do, that would almost guarantee that we catch Ana and can arrest her."

"Yeah, but if someone at the FBI is dirty, then the

whole op could be blown. No, Zach. Between the three of us, we'll be able to do this on our own."

"Do you know how to handle a weapon?" Zach asked.

"I do. I took classes on firearms. For a while, I considered keeping one for protection. But then I decided not to. But I can use one."

"Good, because we're going to get you a gun for this. I'll text Luke and ask him to bring something for you. I assume he is traveling fully loaded."

"Don't worry. I will use it if I need to."

"Unfortunately, that might end up being the case." He wanted to be able to wrap her up and protect her from all of this. But he had to be realistic. They were already going to be outnumbered on this mission. And given all the missing pieces, having her there to corroborate the evidence was vitally important. He couldn't call Brodie and tell him what was going on as much as he wanted to.

"We can do this, Zach. I know we can."

He prayed she was right.

About an hour and a half later, Zach, Jessica and Luke were sitting in Luke's docked boat. Jessica was trying to keep her nerves in check, but her stomach rolled with anticipation.

"All right," Luke said. "I've got supplies for you two, including the night-vision camera and video equipment to ensure we can catch them in the act."

"Thanks for getting this," Zach said. "If we can get

photographic evidence, then that will definitely help to make a case against Ana."

Luke nodded. "I'm going to go down to where the shipment is coming in. It's about a mile from here. I'll text you with updates as I have them. Once I've got eyes on that, then I'll head back up this way and hold down things from here."

"And if nothing happens?" Jessica asked. She wanted to plan for all contingencies.

"Then we regroup and decide how to move forward. But Markov was insistent that his intel was good. And that tonight is the night. Apparently, the operation had been postponed from an earlier date, but he didn't have details on why."

"Maybe that was the chatter we'd heard from Will at Miami PD," Zach said.

"And you asked me to bring a weapon for Jessica," Luke said, opening up his large black bag and pulling out a Glock. "Assuming you know how to use this?" he asked her.

"Yes, I do."

"It's fully loaded, and here's an extra round." He handed her the gun and ammo.

"Thank you." She paused. "And, Luke, please be careful out there."

"Same to the both of you. This will all be over soon." Luke hopped off the back of the boat and headed up the dock to where he'd left his car.

Alone with Zach, Jessica turned to him. "I assume you can drive this boat?"

"Born and raised in Florida on the water. You don't have to worry about that."

She laughed. "Good, because there's plenty of other things."

He took her hand in his. "We'll get through this, Jess. We've come this far."

She nodded as Zach cranked the engine and took the boat out a little bit away from the dock. Jessica enjoyed the feel of the wind blowing against her face. Luke didn't have any old boat. This was a speedboat that packed quite a punch. If they needed to kick it into high gear, at least they'd be able to do so. That gave her some level of comfort.

Jessica knew that the Lord was watching over them. Even as they were headed into the lion's den. But that didn't stop her from uttering another prayer for protection.

Zach slowed down and idled the boat a good ways out from the harbor as they waited to hear from Luke.

The minutes ticked by so slowly. Jessica kept checking her watch and hoping that Luke was okay.

Finally, when Zach's phone started buzzing she jumped.

"It's just Luke texting," Zach said.

"What did he say?" she asked.

"It's go time. The cargo freighter has docked. He says there's a lot of activity at the marina."

More buzzing. More texts.

"Just as Luke predicted," Zach said. "They are unloading into a couple of commercial fishing boats."

"We need to start moving toward Ana's yacht. I've

got the GPS tracker, thanks to Luke's meeting with Markov. It looks like she's also idling a couple of miles from here, off the shore."

"Yes. And we have some lighting from the shore, but it's still dark out here. And I don't want to use our lights that much. But keep your eyes peeled for any other boats. We have to assume that Ana won't be out there alone—she'll have reinforcements. The question is just how many."

Zach skillfully drove the boat toward the blinking GPS light on the tracker. But he made sure they didn't get too close yet. They didn't want to scare off the boats that were actually going to be delivering the product.

Jessica realized that she was digging her fingernails into her clenched fists. She needed to stay alert and help Zach. But to do that she had to stay calm. The wind started whipping up, and she pushed her hair back out of her eyes.

She looked down at the tracker. "Ana's getting closer."

"Yeah. I'm going to stop right here for another minute."

They waited for a few minutes, and then Jessica got the first glimpse of Ana's yacht coming toward them. Two other boats were close by.

"What do we do now?" she asked.

"We need to get closer. But ideally we want to stay under the radar. Get the evidence we can with our night-vision video. We really don't want to engage with them. Once we get the footage we need, then I'll call in backup when I'm sure that the evidence will actually be on the yacht. Because even if there is a turncoat in one of the agencies, they couldn't have infiltrated the entire FBI and the Miami PD."

They moved slowly and quietly toward Ana's yacht. Now there was a lot of activity as the two other large boats got closer.

Jessica found herself holding her breath as she watched the men on the first of the boats start to unload crates and pass them over to the yacht as both ships stilled in the water. She didn't waste any time and started taping the events playing out right before her eyes. The lights from the yacht were bright enough that she felt the footage was going to actually be better than expected. "Can we get any closer?" she asked.

"I'd rather not risk it."

"Just a little bit. If we do, I'm confident we'll get what we need."

"Okay," Zach said, relenting.

But before he could start the engine back up, gunshots rang out through the night.

Zach instinctively dove toward Jessica when he heard the gunshots. He realized that there was another noise that was even more troubling—the unmistakable sound of a boat's motor.

The other speedboat was racing toward them with guns blazing. Not wasting another moment, Zach kicked his engine into high gear. Since they were obviously made, the noise didn't matter. What did matter was trying to get away and getting Jessica to safety.

He was thankful for his college boating days, because he felt comfortable driving in the dark. Yeah, he and his buddies had done some racing years ago. But he'd never been in a high-speed boat chase with a gunman before.

"Stay down low, Jess!" he yelled over the sound of the water splashing up against the side of the boat. He looked back and realized the other boat was gaining ground on them quickly. Luke's boat was no match for the top-of-the-line speedboat chasing them.

Zach tried to think quickly about what their options were, but unfortunately it didn't seem as if they had any. If that boat got to them, they would most likely be killed. *Lord, I need Your intervention right now. Because I don't think I can get us through this on my own.*

"Zach," Jessica screamed. "They're almost on top of us."

He contemplated his next move as beads of sweat mixed with the salty ocean water fell down his face. Maybe if they surrendered, there would be a chance to negotiate for Jessica's life. If he kept trying to outrun them, the gunshots would continue and they both could get shot. Or alternatively, the moment he slowed down they'd both be dead anyway. He did what he thought was best and kept racing forward, but made his course directly toward the yacht. Maybe if they could get on that boat, they'd have some type of chance of getting out alive through some sort of stall or negotiation tactic. Which made him realize that they really needed backup.

"Jess, text Luke and let him know to call in backup ASAP."

"Doing it now." Jessica stayed crouched down low in the boat and used the burner phone to text Luke.

Zach just prayed that some type of help would get to them in time. *Dear Lord, please step in now.*

Suddenly, the boat chasing them started slowing down, but Zach didn't know why. He stayed the course toward the yacht.

"Jess, how good of a swimmer are you?" he asked.

"Not good," she said.

He was hoping as a backup plan he could have her jump out of the boat and just wait for help. But if she wasn't a good swimmer, he couldn't do that. The yacht was absolutely huge. That was their best option.

"Jess, when we get close, I'm going to help you get onto the yacht. Then you need to hide and stay hidden until backup arrives. That's our only chance. We may get a little wet, but I'll be by your side."

"I'll be okay. Where did the other boat go?"

"I'm not sure. Something had to have spooked them. They may have picked up the call for backup. They have to realize we're cornered."

Zach pulled up to the backside of the yacht. The other two boats were at the front. He couldn't tell yet if anyone on the yacht or the other two boats knew they were there. And he had no idea who was all working together and communicating on this op.

"Bring your Glock with you." He idled the boat and got it as close as he safely could. "We're going to have to swim for the boat. I'll have you each step of the way."

"I know you will."

Once again, even though she had admitted that she

wasn't a good swimmer, she wasn't showing an ounce of fear. It was at that moment that he realized how much he loved Jessica.

Jessica took in a huge gulp of salty water as they jumped out of the boat, and she went under for a moment before Zach's strong hands were around her lifting her up. She had been truthful. She wasn't a strong swimmer. But beyond that, she was pretty much a nonexistent swimmer. There had been no family trips to the beach when she was little because she'd never had a real family that cared enough about her to do that. Or anyone to ever teach her how to swim.

But Zach was there as always, providing strength when she was weak. She refused to give up. She knew the Lord would protect them and that His will would be done. Even if that meant that tonight was to be her last night on earth.

"See those rungs over there? I'll boost you up and then I'll follow. But be careful, because once we're on this yacht, we're literally on Ana's home turf. Have your Glock ready and don't hesitate if you feel like your life is threatened. Do you understand?"

She nodded. "Yes. I got it." What had started out as a campaign to gain evidence to prosecute Ana Hernandez had turned into a night where they were fighting for their lives.

As Zach pulled her through the water, she did her best to help, but it seemed as though it would be easier for him to just drag her along than for her to attempt to swim and fight against him. When they got to the edge of the yacht, she looked up at the expansive ship. At least there would be a good possibility she could find somewhere to hide once she got on board.

At this part of the yacht there were different levels, and once Zach hoisted her up she was able to climb up the rungs without much difficulty.

She took a moment to catch her breath to wait for Zach to join her, and that's when she heard the sound of more gunshots.

"Run, Jess!" Zach screamed.

She didn't want to leave him there, but she knew better than to not listen to him. She had to be alive to try to save the both of them. So she ran across the deck and took the first stairway she saw leading down to the next level of the ship.

Her heart pounded as she jogged down the steps and into what looked like a large dining room. Everything was immaculately decorated in navy and ivory surrounding a large table in the center. Jessica needed to find a closet or other hiding place. She couldn't just stand out there like a sitting duck. Her thoughts went to Zach, and she wondered if he was okay. *Lord, please protect Zach.*

There was no closet in the dining room, so she quickly proceeded down the corridor, desperately looking for somewhere to hide.

When she rounded the next corner, she ran right into a man who grabbed on to her arms. She let out a breath when she looked up and saw who it was. "Thank God, it's you. I don't know how you got here so fast, but we really need your help."

As his grip tightened on her arms, she tried to take a step back. He stopped her.

"You should've stayed out of this, Jessica."

As she looked into Ford Cox's eyes, she realized she was staring at the enemy.

FOURTEEN

"Ford, what is going on?" Jessica asked. Although she greatly feared that she knew the answer. He was a dirty FBI agent. And not just any agent, but the special agent in charge of the Miami field office.

"Come on, this way," Ford said.

She cringed as he grabbed tightly on to her arms. Vivid flashbacks of her childhood once again threatened to overtake her. She fought to keep them out of her mind. Now wasn't the time to freak out and lose her cool. He hadn't killed her on the spot, so maybe there was a shred of hope that there was a way out of this.

He led her down another hallway that opened up into a living room. She sucked in a breath as she entered the room and saw that Luke Hernandez was sitting in a wooden chair tied up. This was getting worse by the moment. And she had no idea what had happened to Zach. Was he even still alive?

"What's going on, Ford?" She was going to give it her best shot to keep him talking instead of acting. Luke's dark eyes met her own, and she could tell that he was worried.

Ford sighed loudly as he pulled a gun out of his waistband and pointed it at her. "Take a seat in that other chair. No sudden movements."

She did as he asked because now wasn't the right time to try to make a move. He opened up one of the closet doors and pulled out more rope. She cringed thinking about being tied up. It was too much to handle, and she knew she was on the verge of a panic attack or worse. Once again her past was coming back and threatening to win the battle of wills. *Dear Lord, I need Your strength right now to prop me up. I absolutely cannot do it alone. I'm not strong enough, God.*

She took a few deep breaths as Ford took the rope and secured it around her tightly ensuring that her arms and legs were immobile. Once again she tried to start a conversation with him. "Ford, please. Just tell me what's happening?"

"I tried to keep you out of this, Jessica. I ordered Zach off the case and talked Ian into removing you. I have no idea why you were so insistent on continuing with this vendetta against the Hernandez family."

The Hernandez family must have Ford in their back pocket. "Why are you working with them? They're criminals and you're the head of the FBI field office."

He looked at her with a frown pulling down on his lips. "You are so naive and young. You have no idea what it's really like to do my job day in and day out. Things are never so cut-and-dry like you want to think. Like all the useless stories and ideas they pumped into your head during law school. This is the real world. And this is business. It's not personal."

It felt highly personal to her at the moment, but she was at least getting him to talk so she wanted to keep going. "And Luke?"

"He was a convenient setup that allowed me to meet multiple goals at one time. You and Zach were supposed to focus on him so I could work with Ana and her team. But you decided to go against everything we told you to do. And I hate to say it, but now you're going to have to face the consequences. As much as Ana loves this yacht, there's going to be an unfortunate accident on here tonight."

"But what about the drugs?" she asked. "If you do something to the boat, you'll lose your product."

"We never actually transferred the product onto the yacht. I was prepared for all contingencies. You and Zach just couldn't stand down."

"You know that you can't keep this up forever."

He cocked his head to the side. "You're right. I retire in two years or less. So that's all I need. And once all the dust has settled, it will appear that Luke here is the one who killed you and himself."

"Please, Ford. It doesn't have to be this way."

He walked over to her and knelt down in front of the chair. "There isn't any other option."

"You're making a mistake," Luke said loudly.

Ford stood up and walked over to him. "You realize nothing you could possibly say right now is going to change my mind."

"You think that you've got this all figured out. But you're a loose end, Ford. My father will have absolutely no problem killing you after you kill us. My father always likes to tidy things up."

"Why would he do that? I'm the best thing he has going."

"For now. But you're expendable just like the rest of us."

Ford punched Luke in the face, and Jessica gasped. She struggled against the ropes, but there was no way she could free herself.

"Enough." He turned his gun directly on Jessica, and she screamed. This was it. She was going to die. A loud gunshot rang out.

Zach acted on pure instinct as he pulled the trigger. The gunshot hit Ford in the side of the head. When Zach had seen Ford pull the gun, he couldn't believe his eyes. Ford Cox was working with Ana Hernandez? It was unfathomable. But he'd have time to deal with those details later. He had to free Jessica and Luke right now.

He ran over to where Ford lay on the ground, lifeless. He hadn't had any choice but to take the kill shot. It had either been Ford's life or Jessica's.

Zach ran over to her and started trying to untie her. Just as that was happening, mass chaos broke out as FBI and Miami PD descended on the living room of the yacht. There was yelling and confusion as to why Ford was lying on the ground, shot dead.

It took a few minutes to sort through everything and convince the FBI and Miami PD that Luke and Zach were still the good guys. Once that was settled, Zach turned all his attention to Jessica. The look in her eyes was one of pure terror, and his heart broke for her. He knew she had to be in complete shock after having stared down the face of Ford's gun.

"Jess, are you with me?" he asked as he finished untying the knots.

She nodded and then stood up and threw her arms around him. "I thought I was going to die."

"I know it was terrifying. I'm just so thankful I got in here when I did. I got detained by some of Ana's men outside. But once backup started to get close, they all bailed on one boat to try to get away." He wrapped his arms tightly around her, hugging her close to his body. This woman was everything to him.

"Please don't let me go, Zach."

Nothing could've been sweeter than hearing her say those words. "I'm right here."

"I know I'm a mess and that I've got issues. But if you're willing to work through them with me and be patient, I want to try."

He looked down into her beautiful green eyes and knew his life would never be the same. "It's even more than that, Jess. This has been a crazy journey we've taken together. But in the midst of the danger, we've formed a friendship. One that I value so much. I realized today that I feel much more than friendship for you. I'm totally and madly in love with you, Jess."

Tears started to roll down her cheeks. "Zach, I never thought I'd be able to say this, but I love you, too. With all that I am."

"We need to talk to you," one of the police officers said.

He knew it was important to give his statement, but

there was one more thing he had to do first. He leaned down and kissed Jessica, pressing his lips against hers. Knowing that he'd found the love of his life.

EPILOGUE

Jessica sat on her couch with Tiger snuggled up beside her on one side and Zach on the other. The past nine months had been life changing—but definitely for the better. They had the evidence that they needed to move forward with prosecuting Ana. And it also implicated Mick and Simon. Each family member had hired their own personal lawyers, and it was only a matter of time before one turned on the other two and cut a deal.

It had taken some work, but Luke had been fully vindicated. And he was able to use his fake relationship with Markov to assist the FBI in their ongoing investigation. While Ford's death was regrettable, Jessica was grateful that Zach had acted or she wouldn't be alive. The investigation had shown that Ford had gotten in deep with the Hernandez family and was actively working with them. That's why Ford was so intent on taking down Markov—to be able to help out Mick, who was paying him a handsome sum of money. It bothered Jessica greatly that Ford had decided to work for the Hernandez family, but the experience had made her take off her rose-colored glasses.

In her personal life, she felt content for the first time. Ever. She looked up at Zach, and he smiled at her, melting her heart.

"I have something on my mind," Zach said.

"What's wrong?"

"Absolutely nothing, Jess. That's the thing. I can't remember a time when I was this at peace with my life, and I have you to thank for that. Our partnership has grown into something so much larger than I could have ever imagined."

"I know. I feel the same way."

He grabbed her hands. "There's something else."

"What is it?"

"I have gone over this a lot in my mind, trying to find the perfect timing and perfect words. But then I realized tonight as I looked at you that now is the perfect time. Because it's not about timing or words, it's about the feelings we have between us."

Her heart started beating quicker as she focused on Zach's handsome face.

He moved from the sofa and got down on one knee directly in front of her. Her breath caught as she now understood what he was doing.

"Jess, you're the woman I want to spend the rest of my life with. I never want you to worry about your past being a barrier between us. I think it actually proved to be one of the things that brought us closer together. Seeing your strong faith and perseverance renewed my own. And on this journey together, I have fallen so in love with you, and I know it's a love that is built on a solid foundation."

"I believe that, too."

"So, Jessica Hughes, I have to ask you the most important question I've ever asked in my life." He paused and pulled a ring out of his pocket. A sparkly solitaire diamond symbolizing their great bond. "Will you marry me?"

She knew her answer long before he even asked the question. There was no doubt in her mind. "Yes, Zach. You're the man for me. I want to share a life with you."

Tiger chose that exact moment to move from her side and step onto her lap, and she laughed. "You know I'm a package deal, right?"

"Of course." Zach smiled as he gently slid the ring onto her finger.

She took his hand, and they both stood up. Wrapping her arms tightly around him, she knew that she'd never let go. When his lips met hers, she was ready for a future together with the man who was her partner and true love.

* * * * *

*If you enjoyed this exciting story of suspense
and intrigue, pick up these other stories
from Rachel Dylan*

**OUT OF HIDING
EXPERT WITNESS
PICTURE PERFECT MURDER**

*Available now from Love Inspired Suspense!
Find more great reads at www.LoveInspired.com*

Dear Reader,

Thank you so much for reading. As a lawyer, I loved jumping back into the legal world that I know so well to write this book. And as a Georgia girl who now lives in Michigan, I also enjoyed writing about the warm and sunny setting of South Florida.

Writing characters that are just at the beginning of their careers brought back many memories for me. I can remember the first day I started out as a brand-new attorney in a law firm as clearly as if it were yesterday.

Exploring Jessica's character was an intense but important experience for me. I wanted to show how she could endure such a painful childhood and then turn her life around to fight for others. I found her drive for justice to be inspiring. Her story is a powerful message of faith and perseverance that I hope resonates with you.

I love to hear from readers! You can visit my website at racheldylan.com or email me at racheldylanauthor@gmail.com.

Rachel Dylan

COMING NEXT MONTH FROM
Love Inspired® Suspense

Available August 2, 2016

SECRETS AND LIES
Rookie K-9 Unit • by Shirlee McCoy
When someone tries to kill pregnant teacher Ariel Martin at the local high school, her student's brother, K-9 officer Tristan McKeller, saves her. But can he unravel the secrets in the single mother's past and discover who's after her?

SILENT SABOTAGE
First Responders • by Susan Sleeman
Emily Graves moves to a small town to take over her aunt's bed-and-breakfast...and finds her life in jeopardy. Now if she wants to survive—and save the family business—Emily must turn to Deputy Sheriff Archer Reed for protection.

FATAL VENDETTA • by Sharon Dunn
While reporting on a fire, television journalist Elizabeth Kramer is kidnapped. And with the help of her rival, blogger Zachery Beck, she escapes. Now, as Elizabeth's stalker becomes increasingly violent, Zach is determined to keep her safe.

PLAIN COVER-UP • by Alison Stone
Taking a leave from his job, FBI agent Dylan Hunter expects a chance to relax in a small Amish community—until his former love, Christina Jennings, is attacked. Somebody wants her dead...and she needs his help to stay alive.

DEAD END • by Lisa Phillips
Former CIA agent Nina Holmes is determined to find her mother's killer. And when her investigation puts Nina in danger, she and US marshal Wyatt Ames must solve the murder...or Nina could become a serial killer's next victim.

RANCH REFUGE
Rangers Under Fire • by Virginia Vaughan
When former army ranger Colton Blackwell saves Laura Jackson from an attempted kidnapping, he takes her to his ranch for safety. But when the loan shark trying to collect on her father's debt sends attackers from all directions, will Colton's protection be enough?

LOOK FOR THESE AND OTHER LOVE INSPIRED BOOKS WHEREVER BOOKS ARE SOLD, INCLUDING MOST BOOKSTORES, SUPERMARKETS, DISCOUNT STORES AND DRUGSTORES.

LISCNM0716

Glass shattering.

Rookie K-9 officer Tristan McKeller heard it as he hooked his K-9 partner to a lead. The yellow Lab cocked his head to the side, growling softly.

"What is it, boy?" Tristan asked, scanning the school parking lot. Only one other vehicle was parked there—a shiny black minivan that he knew belonged to Ariel Martin, the teacher he was supposed be meeting with. He was late. Of course. That seemed to be the story of his life this summer. Work was crazy, and his sister was crazier, and finding time to meet with her summer-school teacher? He'd already canceled two previous meetings. He couldn't cancel this one. Not if Mia had any hope of getting through summer school.

He was going to be even later than he'd anticipated, though, because Jesse was still growling, alerted to something that must have to do with the shattering glass.

"Find!" he commanded, and Jesse took off, pulling against the leash in his haste to get to the corner of the building and around it. Trained in arson detection, the dog had an unerring nose for almost anything. Right now, he was on a scent, and Tristan trusted him enough to let him have his head.

Glass glittered on the pavement twenty feet away, and Jesse beelined for it, barking raucously, his tail stiff and high.

A woman appeared in the window. Dark hair. Pale skin. Freckles. Very pregnant belly that wasn't cooperating as she struggled to crawl through the opening. Ariel Martin. The newest teacher at Desert Valley High School. Smart. Enthusiastic. Patient. He'd heard that from more than one parent. He'd even heard it from Mia.

"You okay?" he asked, running to her side.

She shook her head, dark gray eyes wide with shock, a smear of blood on her right hand. She'd cut herself. It looked deep, but she didn't seem to notice. "He's got a gun. He tried to shoot me."

Don't miss SECRETS AND LIES
by Shirlee McCoy, available wherever
Love Inspired® Suspense books and ebooks are sold.

www.LoveInspired.com